Shadow Wind

Diane K. Todd

ACCENT BOOKS
Denver, Colorado

ACCENT BOOKS
A division of Accent Publications, Inc.
12100 West Sixth Avenue
P.O. Box 15337
Denver, Colorado 80215

Copyright © 1990 Accent Publications, Inc.
Printed in the United States of America

Library of Congress Catalog Card Number 89-85992

ISBN 0-89636-259-0

This book is dedicated to my grandmother,
Myrtle G. Maxted,
who taught me what it means to persevere.

Grandma,
I will remember white "choral" bells, slaying thistle dragons, mulberries, bearded irises, violets, and daffodils full of the sun. But, most of all, I will remember you.
I love you, Grandma . . .

McIntyres' was busy, Krista Johnston noted with satisfaction. In the two years since its opening, Krista had seen McIntyres' grow to be the most sought after dining experience in Colorado. She swirled a penstroke under the time Emerson's party of fifteen was to arrive, and replaced the telephone receiver in its cradle.

Glancing across the elegant, modestly lit room with its linen-covered tables resplendent with silver and crystal, Krista spied Jake McIntyre in the far corner. Tall and impeccably dressed, he was speaking with the Stemples—an older couple who were regulars. Krista had been informed earlier by Mr. Stemple that they were celebrating their fiftieth anniversary.

There was a joke in progress between Jake and the older couple. Mrs. Stemple was especially fond of teasing the younger brother of the McIntyre partnership. Even with Jake's back to her, Krista knew the familiar, hands-out gesture that spoke his innocence in whatever the older woman accused.

Krista's gaze shifted to the center of the expansive room to where Darrell McIntyre, senior partner of McIntyres' Eating Establishment, perched in full glory at his ebony baby grand. The raised platform made him a noticeable, albeit pleasantly so, figure.

A smile hinted at Krista's soft, curved lips. She could almost suspect that Darrell had created his restaurant for the benefit of a nightly, captive audience.

The muted tones of the telephone brought Krista back to her job. It was another reservation for a party of ten at 8:00. Krista twisted her mouth in contemplation and consulted her watch. At this rate the second room would have to be opened. And she would have to call for more help.

Glancing up, Krista saw Jake was still at the Stemples' table. She would catch his attention once he left there and inform him of the need to prepare the back room. In the meantime... she flipped open McIntyres' book of telephone numbers and called a handful of extra employees, breathing a sigh of relief when most of them agreed to come in.

Muted traffic noise reached Krista's ears, and she scanned the subtly-lit hall that led to the protected entrance of McIntyres'. A young, stylishly-dressed couple was moving toward her and Krista's squarish jaw unexpectedly tightened.

Instant nausea drained the color from her face. She drew a slow breath against the sudden violence churning in the pit of her stomach.

"Hello, Krista . . . ," the man drawled, dark eyes appraising her as his slow smile exposed a bright expanse of teeth.

Krista lifted her chin as she surveyed the couple. The girl, noticeably apprehensive, clung to his arm. She could not have been more than nineteen or twenty at the most.

Krista's mouth twisted with grim disgust. Her cousin, Steven Mariano, never liked to handle unpleasant business alone. And this would not be pleasant. A thought struck her and her lips pursed against a bark of unuttered, bitter laughter as one brow rose slightly.

As if Steven actually had the capacity to let anything bother his sense of enjoyment.

The girl, Krista noted, was colorless—long, pale blonde hair, pale blue eyes matching her pale blue evening dress... a perfect contrast to Steven's inherited dark looks.

The pen twitched in Krista's fingers, an involuntary quiver.

She deliberately placed the pen alongside the reservation pad, touching it into place with the side of her little finger as she attempted to deal with the chaotic, disjointed thoughts flooding her mind.

Gripping the smooth, wooden edges of the podium, Krista faced the couple, her voice taut with emotion, but low and controlled.

"Go away, Steven. I don't want you here."

"Krista . . ." his voice lowered reprimandingly, "is that any way to greet me after so long a time?"

"McIntyres' is reservation only," Krista countered, tapping the pad on the podium with the tip of her finger. "And since you're not on my list . . ."

"But I am," he smiled. "If you check, you'll find, 'Steven, party of two for 7:45'. Linda and I are a bit early," he studied, then patted the girl's hand that curved about his arm. His glance came back to Krista with a small shrug. ". . . But I thought we could put any troublesome discussion out of the way first. After all, there really is no reason why I shouldn't enjoy my evening once all the unpleasantries are dispensed with."

The initial nausea gave way to a crawling warmth that spread splotches of color along Krista's cheeks. Her reply was dry. "You've never let anything come between you and your pleasure before."

Steven's relaxed smile grew in intensity. "I have no intention of letting it bother me now, either." His expression changed, fractionally serious, "We really do need to talk."

Krista's grey eyes flashed a warning as bright color grew in the planes of her face. "You and I," her finger jabbed at him and back toward herself, "have nothing to discuss."

With a reassuring pat on Linda's fingers, Steven tipped his head toward Krista and questioned, "Do you have any idea how long it took Uncle Anthony to find you?"

"Two years, two months, and five days."

Dark eyebrows raised in modest speculation. "We thought you'd come home." Benign accusation flavored his words. "Who would have dreamed," Steven continued, allowing his glance to absorb the rich decor of McIntyres', "you'd be in a place like this," a grimace accompanied the sudden wave of his hand as he returned his attention to Krista, "doing that."

Krista plucked two menus from the stack. Her hands were shaking. Her low voice was tight with frustrated anger. "It's too bad it didn't take forever," she said, then stopped, spearing her cousin with a look. "Have your dinner, Steven, then get out of my life. Tell Uncle Anthony and Nan the same. I don't want or need you here, and I resent your interference."

Steven sighed. "It's not a matter of what either you or I want, you know. It's what Uncle Anthony says. What he says right now is for you to come home."

With effort Krista schooled herself to a calm pronunciation of her words. "It would not matter if Uncle Anthony were standing here himself. Nothing," she paused for emphasis, "will convince me to return to Mariano Estate."

"You may reconsider your position when you hear what I have to tell you about Uncle Anthony. Surely you can spare a few private moments."

She moved toward the dining area, knowing her cousin and his companion followed. "I have work to do. Have your dinner, then forget you ever saw me."

Krista noted that Jake was moving toward her but was stopped once more by small talk. Krista placed the menus at a secluded nook for two and faced her cousin again.

"Go away, Steven. Don't bother coming back."

"Maybe," Linda spoke softly, hesitantly, her voice as pale as herself, "it would be better for us to wait until later. This might not be the place. . . ."

"You're right," Krista asserted with a sideways, sharply

checked thrust of her hand. Her fingers curled into a ball. "This is not the place. Here, or anywhere else." Her glance flicked over Steven. "Leave it alone," she warned.

Turning, she intercepted a waitress and said, "Carrie, cover for me . . . okay? I'll have Deb and Cheryl take over your tables. Oh," she paused and added, "and tell Jake to open the back room. There are two large parties arriving at 8:00. I've called for reinforcements."

"Sure," Carrie answered, concern shadowing her face. "Are you all right? You look kind of washed out."

Krista took the dinner order Carrie handed her and said, "It's nothing serious. A headache. I'll find some aspirin in the kitchen." Her focus changed and she inclined her head toward the entrance. "There are people waiting to be seated." Catching Carrie's look with a brief flicker of a smile that in no way reached the somber depths of her grey eyes, she added, "Thanks."

Krista gave a firm push on the silent, swinging door to the kitchen. Kneading the tightness at the back of her neck, she reflected momentarily on how serious it might be.

In the kitchen, Krista caught Deb as the uniformed waitress swung through with a new order, and instructed her to take over a portion of Carrie's tables. The waitress's puzzled expression showed her frank curiosity, but Krista did not explain.

Pete, the head cook, was a bit surprised at Krista's appearance in the kitchen at this early hour, but said nothing more than an upraised eyebrow could insinuate. Giving her hands a quick wash and dry, Krista grabbed salad plates and began to fill them. Once she had Stephanie's order started, she would corner Cheryl and give instructions for the remaining tables.

Pausing, Krista pressed the shaky heel of her hand into her forehead where a frown etched itself between her brows. She would have to find some aspirin, too.

A bright splash of dressing splattered the counter. Krista drew her breath slowly through her teeth and grabbed a cloth to swipe at the oily mess. Dumping dressing onto two more salads, she shoved the ladle back into its container and reached for the croutons . . . only to be stopped by Jake's strong hand enclosing hers.

"You're shaking," he said, greenish-grey eyes surveying her face as she glanced upward, surprised, into his. "Leave that. Deb can take care of it. Come on." Jake gave her a gentle, but determined shove toward his back office. "I'd say you need to sit down."

"Cheryl hasn't been told to cover for Carrie."

"I'll take care of that," Jake replied and pushed open the office door with the flat of his hand.

Jake's office was a cluttered cubicle in which he had somehow managed to arrange a large desk, a small loveseat and a stuffed chair, decorated by the various odds and ends of everyday life. He indicated the worn, tweedy chair with a lift of his chin and ordered, "Sit. I'll be back with coffee."

With a brief backward look, Jake tugged the door closed to offer Krista privacy from the kitchen noise.

Removing a tie and shirt from the back of the chair, Krista laid them over the end of the clothes-draped and magazine-piled loveseat. For all his fastidiousness where the restaurant was concerned, Jake was definitely more relaxed when it came to his own domain. Jake's walls were lined with certificates and pictures, his desk scattered with papers and books, including his Bible. It was open, as it always seemed to be whenever she entered this room.

Krista sank into the high-sided chair and leaned her head against the padded back. She gave a sigh and touched her temples with the tips of her fingers, pressuring tiny circular patterns into the pain that was growing there.

Krista adjusted her fingertips, avoiding the nagging reminder that her own two-month-old Bible hadn't been opened much lately. She allowed her eyes to be drawn to the portraits hanging on the walls. There were family pictures of all five McIntyre brothers and their sister, carbon copies of one another with fair hair and greenish-grey eyes. All were athletic, evidenced by the many sports-oriented shots. And they all had a mischievous gleam in their eyes.

"Here we are." Jake breezed into the room carrying two steaming cups of coffee and kicked the door shut with his heel. His eyebrows rose, taking note of the action of her fingertips. "Bad one, huh?" he asked.

"Violent," Krista murmured, and raked her nails through her shoulder length hair. It was brown, straight—none of the Mariano wave.

Sliding the cups onto two reasonably clear spots on his desk, Jake fished around in one of the desk's cluttered drawers and came up with a bottle of aspirin. "I wish," he said "you wouldn't come to work if you don't feel well." He popped the lid and handed Krista two tablets.

"I'm fine." She accepted the offered cup of coffee and swallowed the aspirins, scalding the back of her throat as she did so. "It's just," she swallowed again, clearing her throat at the stinging sensation, "a tension headache."

Jake shuffled papers, closed his Bible, and perched on the edge of his desk. His eyebrows rose with an unasked question.

Krista hesitated, studied the edge of her cup, then looked at him and shook her head. "I'd rather not go into it," she said.

"Hey, I won't pry." Jake McIntyre lifted his cup to his lips. "What's your business is your business. But I would hope you'd come to me if something is bothering you." Jake shrugged, a lift coming to his brows. "It's not like you to walk off the floor like that."

Rubbing her finger along the curve of her mouth, Krista

considered her boss for several seconds. "Thanks," she said, her hand dropping to wrap around her mug, "but there will be no true confessions tonight."

He gave a nod of acceptance, took another drink from his cup and settled the sturdy kitchen crockery on his desk. "Will you be all right for awhile?" he asked. "I have to check on a couple of things and then I'll come back."

Krista rose and placed her cup alongside his. "I need to return to the floor. We're short-handed."

"Forget it, lady." His fingers circled her wrist and she glanced up, surprised. "You're going to take at least a half-hour break to give those aspirins a chance to take effect."

"Jake. . ." she began.

His brows rose. "Krista. . ." His voice was a slight imitation of hers. "You heard what I said."

Sliding to his feet, Jake moved toward a closet where he rummaged on the shelf for a blanket and pillow. "Kick off your shoes," he ordered over his shoulder. The pillow was tossed at one end of the loveseat, and the precariously folded blanket dangled from his arm. He removed miscellaneous articles into scattered piles.

Shaking the folds from the blanket, Jake waited for Krista to step obediently out of her pumps.

The loveseat was as threadbare as the chair, and as comfortable, although a bit cramped. Jake fluttered the blanket and settled it over Krista as she laid down.

"I called Darla," she informed him, rubbing a mote of fluff from her nose with a swipe of her hand. "Daina, too, and Trish. They should be here anytime."

"Good girl. I'll be back to check on you. Stay put for at least half an hour."

Turning to walk out of the room, Jake stopped when Krista spoke his name.

With a tiny smile on her lips, she asked, "Don't you ever finish a cup of coffee?"

Jake grinned, his hand resting on the doorknob. "Only at 2:00 a.m."

She murmured a derisive acknowledgment to which Jake's grin shifted knowingly. He opened the door.

"Jake. . ."

"What?"

"Please let me know if the couple at table seventeen leaves early."

Jake's eyes narrowed slightly. As he began to close the door, he stopped, "I'll come tell you if they leave within the next thirty minutes."

Jake left, the door clicking solidly behind him.

Krista stared at the back of the door, swirls of dark wood forming shapes of faces and figures. . .provoking thoughts she wanted to forget.

A tiny moan escaped from between her suddenly stiffened lips. She curled her knees to her chest, ignoring the damage she was doing to her dress.

Beyond the door she could hear the sounds of the kitchen personnel filling orders. Everyone working, doing his job—a part of the McIntyre family.

And she was in here. Her gaze flicked around the room, her throat tightening. She closed her eyes.

"Dear God," Krista whispered in uncertain anguish, "what am I going to do now?"

—2—

It was quiet...except for a slight rustling of paper...a sound that caught Krista's attention, drawing her mind into focus with a curious wonder of where she was, followed almost immediately with thoughts of Steven.

She suppressed the urge to groan and slowly opened her eyes.

Jake sat at his desk in a yellow circle of light that glowed from the swing-arm lamp positioned over the Bible he was studying. He had a pen in his hand; his collar was unbuttoned, tie and jacket discarded, vest open. A curl of steam rose from the coffee cup placed near his right hand. The other cups, hers and his, remained where they had been placed earlier that evening.

Blinking her eyes to clear her sleep-drugged senses, Krista watched Jake, his fingers stroking his brow as he silently closed his eyes. He remained that way for quite a while. Eventually he glanced up and saw Krista watching him.

It was very quiet and the lack of noise itself prompted Krista to ask, in a husky, sleep-deepened voice, "What time is it?"

Jake consulted his watch. "1:42." The corner of his mouth rose. "I'll finish this cup of coffee."

In spite of herself, Krista gave a half-twisted smile. "You never do," she said, her voice stronger as she slid around so that her feet touched the floor. Her toes wiggled the blanket into place. "I think you like coffee just because it smells good."

Jake tossed his pen on the desktop and the swivel chair creaked as he stretched his hands in a comfortable motion above his head. "You've found me out," he said. "Promise you won't tell Pete? He goes to great pains to make my coffee 'just the way I like it'."

"I promise. Why did you let me sleep?"

"Who am I to awaken Sleeping Beauty?"

Krista's lips compressed, eyes narrowing. "When did Steven finally leave? I assume my cousin introduced himself."

"We had a chat," Jake admitted. His forearms rested on the desk. "Mr. Mariano explained a few things about you two."

"Such as?"

"He said you'd been raised together—that his and your parents died in a skiing accident when you were both two-years-old. From the way he talks, he thinks the world of you. . . even expressed some anxiety over your well-being."

"Ha!" Her voice was a sharp exclamation, one she could not prevent, that mirrored the immediate disdain on her face. "Steven thinks only of himself and what he can buy or do or who. . ."

"Krista. . ." Jake retrieved his pen and leaned back, a leisurely motion that caused his face to be shadowed, away from the direct glare of the lamp. She could see him draw the pen slowly through his fingers, balancing it between his fingertips, the light playing on the gold casing.

"Why didn't you tell me your name was Mariano?"

Self-justified anger registered in the widening of Krista's grey eyes. "Because it isn't."

"Mr. Mariano said it was. He made certain I knew of the Mariano reputation." His quiet voice spoke matter-of-factly. "Because of your uncle you're worth millions." The pen directed itself at her. "Is that something to be ashamed of?"

"My name is Krista Johnston . . . full name Krista M.—for

15

Mariano—Johnston, to be exact." She sighed heavily. "I don't need the Mariano name to get by, Jake. In fact, I prefer, as you may have realized, that I not consider the unfortunate fact of my Mariano lineage. Johnston does me quite well. I choose to leave it that way."

A minute shrug shifted Jake's shoulders. The pen was laid on his desk, and his face was no longer shadowed. "I'm sorry. It's really none of my business."

"Forget it. There's more going on here than you could possibly understand, Jake. I just don't want to delve into things that are over and done with."

Jake levered his eyebrows upwards. "I got the impression your cousin will take exception to that opinion."

"That would be nothing new. We've been at odds ever since I can remember."

"He asked for your address and phone number."

Krista stiffened. "You didn't. . ."

"No." Jake's forefinger ran alongside his nose, accompanied by a conceding lift of his shoulders. "He was persuasive, in a not too rude sort of way, but he accepted my disinclination as a policy of McIntyres'."

"Not that it will stop them," Krista murmured more to herself than to Jake.

"Them?"

Her mouth opened, then closed. Krista shook her head once, briefly. Pushing the blanket aside she said, "I have to go home."

"Want me to take you?"

Krista reached for her shoes and slipped them on one at a time. "If you took me home, I'd be without transportation in the morning."

A grin caught the corner of Jake's lips. "I could pick you up for brunch."

"Thanks all the same, but. . ."

". . .Some other time."

Krista avoided his look, rose, and took a few steps to the open doorway. Her hand touched the doorjamb. She stopped when Jake's voice arrested her movements.

"Another thing. . ."

"What?" Krista asked.

"Don't leave the Lord out of whatever is happening right now. God is able to take care of it. Remember that."

Looking back briefly, Krista caught the seriousness reflected in Jake's eyes. "I know," she replied, her voice quiet.

"I'll call in forty-five minutes. . .just to make sure you've gotten home okay. That back road to your house bothers me. Especially at night."

"If you'd like," she agreed, "I should be there by then."

Krista walked into the kitchen. A prickly feeling enveloped her as her footsteps echoed on the scoured tile. Retrieving her purse from her mini-locker off to the side of the vacant kitchen, she made her way through the main dining area. She rummaged in her purse for McIntyres' keys, unlocked the front door, and let herself out. Relocking it, she started toward her burgundy sports car, sitting at the far end of the parking lot beside Jake's dark Porsche. Theirs and the cleaning van were the only vehicles left on the lot.

Traffic passed by sporadically and a police siren could be heard wailing in the distance. A large car moved slowly under the streetlamps along the side road, its dark paint glistening in each passing circle of light. She eased her car onto the street and toward the Interstate.

As much as Krista loved Denver, she loved the mountains even more, seeing them as a refuge. After leaving Mariano Estate on the coast of northern California, she had escaped to Colorado with the hope of never being bothered again by her uncle and former guardian, Anthony Mariano. She should have known better than to hope.

When Krista came to her turnoff, she signaled and exited

the highway, driving along the dark, narrow, two-lane graveled road toward her house. Another car swung in behind her, and Krista adjusted her rearview mirror against the intense glare of the headlights. Her car leapt forward on a straight stretch, the vehicle responding well to her touch, and the headlights fell behind.

The home she had found was off main roads, far enough from the city to be frequented by visitors from the surrounding forest. That was one of the reasons she had chosen it. Her home was her sanctuary from all she had left behind.

She supposed, grimly thinking back over the intervening years since leaving California, she had prepared herself for the inevitable. Still, she wondered, how does one prevent impending disaster? Uncle Anthony, she knew, would not reconsider his position once he had found her. . .and he had. Somehow, someway she had to be ready.

Krista's teeth set as she shifted through an upward curve in the road, jamming the gears with a hard thrust of the palm of her hand. The car behind had caught up, following closely in her dust trail. She wished the person would either pass or slow down to permit more space between them.

Was asking to be left alone too much? After all that Uncle Anthony and Nan, her childhood disciplinarian and the estate housekeeper, had subjected her to, couldn't they respect her privacy? Her fingers tightened on the wheel. The sports car's headlights bobbed in a sweeping arc across the pines as she hugged the next tight curve, and the car behind her surged forward on her left. Krista heard the gunned engine roar as the large car drew even with her. Glancing sideways, her eyes widened at the vehicle's closeness.

Krista instinctively slowed. The other car swept forward, then swerved deliberately into her path!

Krista gasped harshly. Slamming the brake, she jerked the wheel to the right. Her tiny car spun to the outside of the graveled road, barely missing the larger car. She slid along the edge. The ditch, black and ominous, opened before her.

Krista heard a thin cry and knew it had come from her lips. Her hands clenched the wheel, and she snapped it back toward the middle of the road. The car skidded sideways. A sharp cry of fear escaped her throat as she heard the tires skate on the crumbling edge of the road. Then the engine stalled, and the car ground to a stop.

The large, dark car sped ahead, racing up the road and out of sight around a curve of trees. Krista stared in shocked disbelief at the vanishing red glow of taillights.

The silence of the mountain night enveloped her. Clouds of dust drifted, curling through the beams of her lights, forming ghostly figures that wrapped themselves about her car with grasping, sinister tendrils.

Hands still clutching the wheel, she dropped her forehead to rest on her knuckles. Her nerves trembled, half in fear, half in impotent anger. Then lifting her head, she drew a ragged breath, eyes widening as harsh realization struck.

Someone had tried to kill her!

—3—

The phone was ringing as Krista mounted the steps to the deck that surrounded her rustic, contemporary home. The shrill vibration grated her raw nerves, and she hurried to slide the key in the lock of the heavy wooden door. Her fingers fumbled and, with an exasperated exclamation, she shoved the door open. Slapping at the switch just inside the door put her living room in the dim glow of a lamp on the end table.

Krista snatched the receiver from where the telephone sat next to the lamp. She sucked in a breath, and her "hello" echoed her fear.

There was a space of silence on the other end. Finally, Jake said, "I was getting worried."

Krista dropped her purse on the white, knobby-weave sofa and raked her nails through her hair.

"Jake, someone just tried to run me off the road."

"*What?*"

"A car—a big one. He swerved right in front of me. I'm certain he tried to run me off the road."

"But. . .*why?*"

"I don't know. I can't imagine why."

"Do you want me to come out?"

"No," Krista's head shook. "No, don't do that. I'm okay. I'm shaky," she stared at the trembling of her free hand, then tucked it under her other arm, hugging herself in an effort to still her quivering, "but I'll be all right."

"I think you should report it to the police."

"No!" Krista said abruptly, then added before he could say anything more, "Jake, I have an awful lot to think about. I'll see you at work tomorrow."

She hung up before he could reply.

The past few hours had been worthless. Why Krista dressed for bed and went to the trouble of pulling down the sheets, she did not know. Thoughts of what had happened, what was about to happen, and the action she should take whirled around and around in her head.

Who had tried to run her off the road. . .and why? Then, what was she going to do about Uncle Anthony?

She was tired. More than that, she felt defeated even before the contest of wills between her and her uncle began.

Now that Uncle Anthony and Nan knew where she was, she had no doubt they would try to take action—to force her back to Mariano Estate.

She did not want to go back. But could she stay here?

She thought of Jake, of McIntyres', of who she was now and . . .why would someone want to hurt her or. . .*kill* her?

Krista shifted between the sheets in a restless movement, then tossed the bedcovers off. The hardwood floors were cool beneath her bare feet as she padded her way into the living room.

A massive picture window she stubbornly refused to cover provided a spectacular view of the surrounding valley and jagged mountains. Already the rising sun was beating back the morning mists from the rolling, pine-covered hills. It would be another hot day.

Going to the sliding glass doors off the eating area next to the kitchen, Krista walked out onto the deck, the wooden surface slightly damp under her feet. She breathed in the spiciness of the surrounding trees and attempted to coax back the sense of solace God's creation gave her.

The telephone rang and Krista stepped back through the

open door. She debated, then, when it rang once more, lifted the receiver.

Jake's voice greeted her. "Did I wake you?"

"No."

"I thought maybe I wouldn't. Did you get any sleep?"

"Only what I got at McIntyres'." Krista shifted her stance. "How about yourself? This is early even for you."

"I've been at the office all night. Still am, in fact. How are you doing this morning?"

Flickering memories of Steven's face and vanishing taillights slipped through her mind. She flinched away from the thoughts. "As well as can be expected, I suppose."

"Have you had breakfast?"

The question drew a slight smile to Krista's lips. "What do you think?" she asked.

"I think breakfast will be delivered inside, say, an hour? Does that give you enough time to pull yourself together and fix a pot of coffee?"

"Can you bring some fruit? Any kind. You know I'm not picky."

A smile crept into Jake's voice. "I'll see what I can do."

After hanging up the telephone, Krista took time for a quick shower and changed into a grey-blue printed cotton blouse and skirt outfit that leant color to her soft eyes. She added a pair of white, slip-on canvas shoes, then spent a few moments adjusting odds and ends about her house. When she straightened her Bible on her nightstand, she stopped. Picking it up, Krista stared at the dark cover with its gold lettering, then ran the palm of her hand over the grained leather. She turned to the flyleaf and read the words Jake had inscribed.

"Trust in the Lord with all your heart, and do lean not on your own understanding. In all your ways acknowledge Him, and He will make your paths straight." Proverbs 3:5-6

Krista carefully folded the cover back into place and laid it down.

The smell of heat and dust touched her nose when Krista walked out to the porch after hearing Jake's car pull into the driveway.

Krista leaned her elbows on the railing and watched Jake's jeans clad figure lift a sack from his Porsche. She did not know how he found time to acquire a tan with his working hours, but somehow he managed to maintain a dark, golden hue. Sunlight flashed gold from the hair on his arms, mimicking the color of the hair on his head.

Krista found herself admiring him. He looked good. Perhaps. . .she should not put him off like she had in the past. He was a very special person. She knew she could trust him.

But. . .she gave herself a mental shake. Now was not the time to permit the beginning of a serious relationship. Not with Steven in the state and Uncle Anthony privy to her whereabouts. . .and strange cars attempting to run her off the road. She frowned. It would be better, for both of them, to resist that thought. . .as she had, for the most part, the past two years.

"You made good time," Krista said as Jake mounted the stairs.

"I'm hungry," Jake replied, studying her. He smiled and shifted the sack in his arms so that his hand rested briefly on Krista's shoulder.

Ignoring the front door, they circled the deck and entered the bright, open kitchen by way of the sliding doors.

Krista eyed the sack. "I'm starving. What did you bring?"

"Food," Jake said, setting his burden on the counter. The one word was emphasized by the rattle of the sack as Jake removed a cantaloupe from the bottom of the bag and tossed it with nonchalance from one hand to the other. His eyebrow rose. "Will you cut it or shall I?"

"I will," Krista replied, taking the rough-veined melon from his hand. "You can scramble the eggs."

Jake's face evolved into a suspicious gleam. "How'd you know I brought eggs?"

Laying the cutting board on the countertop, Krista rummaged in the drawer for a long-bladed knife and said, "You always do."

"You make it sound as if I bring breakfast to you all the time."

"Okay," she relented with an incline of her head. "So you've only brought breakfast two times. . ."

"This is the third."

"Three times, " she corrected herself. "Anyway, it's always been eggs."

Jake make a noncommittal sound along with a shrug of his shoulders and dug out a sack of croissants. . .and a carton of eggs. "I hope you have some juice," he said. "I forgot to bring some. Besides," he backtracked on the conversation, "I like eggs."

"I do have juice," Krista replied. The knife blade bit deep into the flesh of the melon, slicing it neatly in half. "And I like eggs, too."

"So that's settled." Blond brows lifted in accordance with the upward curve of his lips.

Jake spoke again. "Steven Mariano called the restaurant this morning—just after I talked with you. Caught me as I was heading out the door."

Hands stilled and grey eyes focused on Jake. "What did he want?"

"More information about you and, no," Jake's answer interrupted her question as he leaned back against the counter, fingers busy creasing the folds of the sack. "I told you I wouldn't tell him anything, didn't I?"

"You did. But you may as well realize," the knife tip lifted into the air and Krista directed it slightly toward Jake before returning to her task, "he won't quit. Motivated Marianos don't quit. And I'm certain," two rocking quarters of melon lay where a half had been a scant second before, "Steven has more motivation than he can keep up with. In fact, I wouldn't be at all surprised if he were on his way here right now, in spite of your noble intentions of protecting my whereabouts."

Laying the sack on the counter, Jake reached for Krista, grasping her shoulders so that she turned to face him. His green eyes narrowed and darkened. His voice was low, all hint of fun erased from his features as he surveyed Krista's serious face.

"What's going on?" he asked. "First your family, then the car last night."

"I don't know about the car," she answered truthfully.

"What about Steven?"

Lips compressing, Krista glanced at the knife she still held in her hand. She sighed and laid the knife on the cutting board, saying, "He's the least of my worries."

Slipping from Jake's grasp, Krista edged away.

"I know you want to help, Jake, but the best thing you can do is leave me alone. I appreciate your efforts, but I'll have to take care of my own problems." Krista squeezed her eyes shut for a moment, then sighed again, a resolute lift coming to her chin, along with a tiny shake of her head. "You don't want to get messed up with me, Jake. I've got more problems right now than you'd care to deal with. Find someone whose life isn't so complicated—someone able to appreciate how. . . special you are and," her voice colored with regret, "can return that to you."

"And you can't? Don't shut me out, Krista. We've shared work and fun times together—gone places, done things. Trust me," he said, "with whatever these problems are. Let me help."

Her glance swept over Jake's intent features. Since Steven's arrival she had known it was time to face what she had run away from two years ago. But to involve Jake? And now, with the perplexing possibility of someone trying to hurt her, there was even more for her to consider.

Krista propped herself against the counter with the heels of her hands behind her so she could see beyond the room.

The day had grown quickly hot. The late summer sun shimmered on the hills outside the kitchen doors, turning the grasses brown beneath and around the tall pines. Even the trees themselves appeared to have lost color underneath their coating of dust.

Heat. Pressure. She frowned and considered her options. . . which were few under the circumstances. She loved Colorado and its dramatic change of seasons. . .and it made her ill to think of losing what she had here. She had so much and now. . . .

"Krista?"

Her gaze came slowly back to Jake and refocused on the question in his eyes. It was funny how they darkened to deep, pine green whenever he was serious, like now.

Krista opened her mouth and drew a soft breath. "I haven't the right to involve you," she said. "There could be serious repercussions."

"Why don't you let me decide that for myself?"

Krista studied the man who was her boss, the man who had become the closest person she had to a friend. Krista slid her forefinger along the edge of the countertop and studied the imaginary line she traced. She sighed and was honest with herself; she did want Jake to know.

"You're right," Krista began slowly, still studying the movement of her hand, "when you suggest it's a 'who' rather than a 'what'—although Steven is hardly a threat," she added, drawling somewhat as the side of her mouth twisted. "My uncle, Anthony Mariano, is . . . a difficult man, at best." Her fingers splayed on the cool countertop, and she swiveled her

26

head to face Jake. "Uncle Anthony has interfered with my life all of my life. He's demanding—wanting his way, expecting me to fall into his plans, and, now that he knows where to locate me, it will start all over again."

Jake waited, leaning back against the cabinets as he studied Krista and listened to her words.

"He's a manipulator," she added, "full of expectations of who and what I am." Krista sucked the corner of her mouth as she paused, drew on her thoughts. "I left all that two years ago when I realized the impossibility of me carrying out his designs for my life."

"That's when you came to work for McIntyres'."

Krista nodded.

"Did you try telling your uncle how you felt?"

The short, quiet exclamation could have been mistaken for laughter. She shook her head. "You don't understand." The suggestion of a smile that touched her lips did not veil the seriousness that darkened the color of her eyes. She said, "You don't *tell* Uncle Anthony anything. *He* tells *you*."

The telephone rang—a shrill, startling sound that stopped Krista's words, changing her expression to one of poorly masked anger.

Instinctively she knew who the early morning caller would be. And answering it would thrust her headlong into events she wanted no part of.

—4—

Krista's stomach began to churn with sudden vehemence, and she wondered if she was going to be ill. She knew the color had gone from her face and the dead, dull feeling she had never forgotten sank deep in the pit of her stomach.

The instrument rang again, four, five times.

Puzzled, Jake asked, "Are you expecting that call?"

"I have been since last night."

"You're not going to answer it?"

"No."

"Is it your uncle?"

"Or Nan," Krista said and added at Jake's uncomprehending look, "the housekeeper."

"What if I answered it?"

Krista's fingertips touched her lips. They had gone icy.

"I get the impression," Jake continued, "that these people will not leave you alone until you've made it clear that you refuse to be bothered."

Krista's voice whispered from between her fingers. "I'm not. . .prepared to do that."

Jake gave her a measured look. "Let me answer and see what happens."

Krista did not reply.

Jake turned in one swift movement and strode purposefully through the rooms. He touched the phone and looked back across the open space to where Krista stood in the kitchen.

Krista snagged her lower lip, nipping it between her teeth as

Jake lifted the receiver.

"Hello," Jake spoke. "Yes, it is. . . .Yes, she is." His look sought Krista's and held it. "May I ask who's calling?" There was a pause. "Just a moment."

Placing his hand over the mouthpiece, Jake said, "It is Nan Carr, your uncle's housekeeper."

"I don't want to talk to her," Krista spoke with a trembling firmness. Her hands had begun to slide up and down her arms as if warding off a sudden chill, her fingertips tightening at intervals as they moved. "Tell her . . . I don't want to talk to her."

Jake's mouth twisted sideways, and he spoke to the caller. His gaze, however, remained on Krista.

Krista, with mammoth effort, stilled her restless hands. She could feel Jake's penetrating study, as she attempted to decipher what it was about her former housekeeper that upset her so much. How could she explain the essence of subtlety about the Estate? The constant, innocuous-seeming little things?

Jake's voice was firm as he told the housekeeper, "Krista does not want to speak with you. I can give her the message if there is something important she needs to know." He halted for a space of time, "I see. . . .No, I understand." A frown crept between his brows as he listened.

Jake blocked his words to the housekeeper by once again laying his palm over the mouthpiece. He hesitated, as if torn between the words of the woman he had just spoken to and the obvious distress Krista was enduring. He said to Krista, "I think you'd better talk to her. She has a few things she needs to tell you."

Krista's head moved from side to side. The churning in her stomach subsided fractionally through sheer will, but she could only stare at Jake.

Running her fingertips up the edges of her cheekbones to her temples, Krista's voice deteriorated to an anguished whisper. "I can't."

In a quiet, speculative tone Jake replied, "No one likes to face unpleasant situations, but you really do need to talk to her and hear what she has to say." His lips tightened a touch, then softened as one eyebrow slid encouragingly upward at his private thoughts. "She doesn't sound too formidable."

Krista's grey eyes darkened to slate. Her voice became strangely void of emotion.

"Nan never did."

Jake waited. Krista could see the conflicting emotions crossing his face. What Nan had said had made a serious impression on him.

She shuddered.

Numbly traversing the intervening space between her and Jake, Krista held out her hand. Then she looked up at him, realizing the difficulty he had in handing the receiver to her.

Taking a steadying, determined breath, Krista said, "Hello, Nan."

Long distance hum sounded in Krista's ear, and she could see Nan in her mind's eye—diminutive, orderly, with a delicate sort of attraction.

Mariano Estate's housekeeper spoke earnestly, "Krista. . . child, it's been so long. We've been so worried. I never thought I'd hear your voice again."

And I hoped I would never have to hear yours. "What do you want?" The words were evenly spaced, toneless. Krista could feel Jake's attentive watchfulness. She turned her back on him, stepping away when he would have offered encouragement through his touch, her shoulders rounded as if warding off a blow.

Nan's voice was soft. But, then, it always had been soft. Krista could never remember when Nan had spoken harshly or in anything but a moderate tone.

"It's your uncle," the housekeeper was saying. "He asked me to call."

"He always preferred you handle those 'small' details."

Silence—to Krista, condemning silence—filled the line. Nan's silences were always condemning.

"There is no easy way to say this," Nan continued, hesitating somewhat, her voice trailing to a whisper before rising in compelling intensity. "Your uncle...is very ill, Krista. We are all...concerned for his health. He has not been well this past year. He wants to see you. He has asked to see you. Please."

There was a semblance of begging in that last word that momentarily surprised Krista into silence. When had Nan ever *requested* anything of her?

"Come home," the housekeeper said.

Krista's jaw set with a fierceness that sent an ache throbbing upward through her temples. Face twisting in angry agony at the command from Nan, she squeezed her eyes shut. Anthony Mariano would somehow find a way—any way—to force her presence at Mariano Estate. The man had tentacles. They grasped and smothered and. . . .

"This may be hard for you to understand, Nan, but I'm not leaving Colorado. This is where I live, and I hope to never see Uncle Anthony or Mariano Estate again."

"Child, he only did what he felt was right for you."

Eyes snapping open, Krista retorted, "That's all he did all of my life—what *he* felt. Did either one of you ever bother to ask me what *I* felt. . .what I wanted. . .what I *needed?*"

Krista shook her head vehemently, trembling fingers covering her compressed lips, refusing to lash out and accuse further. She had to maintain control of herself. The worst thing she could do was to lose control.

Nan was saying, "We didn't realize you had taken it so hard. You stayed and finished your education."

"I finished the last two weeks of my master's degree because I needed to finish what I'd started. Krista *Johnston*, magna cum laude. Remember? Not Mariano. Besides, it took me that long to arrange my finances and make my plans." She added, "I had hoped you would never find me."

"We thought. . .you had seen reason."

"Reason?" Krista's voice became deathly quiet. "You take away the most vital part of my life and you call that reason?"

In the split second that followed, Krista could visualize Nan regrouping, gathering herself for the next softly spoken battle, and Krista steeled her will against the words.

"Think of your sense of responsibility, then," the housekeeper stressed patiently. "You owe your uncle that much. He is very ill. We are worried. What can one more visit hurt?"

What could it hurt?

Krista flinched at the jab of pain the very thought caused.

Krista's cadence had a flat, harsh quality to it. "I've heard of responsibility all my life—obligations, upholding the Mariano reputation." She took a breath. "I'm not a Mariano or anything the name implies. My name is Johnston. Leave me alone, Nan. Call off Steven. I have my own life to live, and I don't want you or Steven or Uncle Anthony fouling it up for me."

"Please, Krista. . ."

"Tell Uncle Anthony," her head shook as she vainly searched for words, ". . .I'm sorry. I can't go back there. I don't expect either of you to understand," she took a breath, "but don't call back, Nan."

—5—

Krista broke the connection with a finality that seemed to echo in her silent house. Following the length of cord to the wall, she knelt and jerked the plug, severing any possible link to the house over a thousand miles away.

Krista slid her hands over her face, trying to alleviate the dead, chilled feeling.

What was she going to do? She could not hide anymore, hoping they would not find her. They had this time. They would again.

It was then she remembered Jake, and she raised her pale face to see him silently watching her actions.

Shame flooded over her and lent wings to her feet. She shot past Jake's surprised form, intent only on escaping his pained, uncomprehending expression.

She had to be alone. To think. Her world was falling in like an unstable house of straw, and she needed desperately to steady its foundation.

The front door slammed in unison with Jake's shout calling her name.

Her feet sprang swiftly along the wooden porch and vibrated the staircase as she raced down the stairs.

Realizing she had left her car keys in the house, she cut through the forest growth that bordered her home and disappeared among the trees, racing along a barely discernible path.

She ducked, low hanging pine boughs brushing their scratchy needles at her face.

She had grown soft, she admitted to herself. The months away had chipped her armor. It had taken so little to shake her. She was behaving badly and Jake, the last person she wanted to see her out of control, was a witness to her complete instability where Uncle Anthony was concerned.

Her breathing was labored, more from fear and frustration and her efforts not to cry, than the length of her run.

Krista stopped and gasped, thrusting her weight against the creased bark of an aged pine. Her head hung and she crumpled to her knees, then flopped backward, twisting so that her back connected with the tree trunk.

Strands of her hair snagged in the bark. Her fingers were tight-knuckled fists lying impotently in her lap.

Hard as she tried not to, tears seeped from beneath her tightly closed lids as despair washed through her. There was no escaping now. She had no more time left.

Unable to stem the flow, tears ran unchecked down either side of her face. Anger, hurt, and defeat flowed with them. Gradually, Krista was overcome with an emotionless acceptance of the situation. Short of running away again, she knew there was nothing she could do. And today had proven how futile that idea was.

The onslaught of tears dried on her face as a welcome, cooling breeze whispered through the brush, and still she remained where she was.

Propriety dictated that she return to the house and apologize to Jake. . .if he were still there to apologize to.

A painful frown touched her face when the thought that he might not be there crossed her mind, but she could not will her deadened body to move.

A bird trilled in the tree above her, and she unthinkingly searched out the song, but could not discover its source. A small, grey squirrel chattered noisily and flitted along a low-hanging branch. Pine needles scattered with his passing. When a twig snapped, Krista drew her chin down to study her fingers, stiff and white, uncurling slowly in her lap.

It was Jake. She was aware of his presence and accepted it, realizing without words that he accepted her silence until she was ready to speak.

Squatting on his heels in front of her, Jake examined her tear-stained face and she bore his scrutiny, her own glance flicking over the planes of his features, stopping to see the depths of his eyes.

She owed him something. . .some sort of explanation.

"When I was a little girl," she started, her voice clear in the heated air, "I used to run away from home."

Krista altered her gaze to a point over Jake's left shoulder where a patch of blue was perfectly framed by the pine boughs of several close-growing trees.

"After my parents died, I lived with my uncle in his huge, beautiful mansion on a peninsula along the northern California coast. It was built up on a cliff with a view of the waves pounding the rocks below. And I used to run away." Her brow creased in memory. "Whenever I felt no one loved me or understood me or cared. . .whenever things didn't go right and I couldn't do anything about it, I would disappear.

"The first few times I ran away, I could hear the servants calling my name, but I wouldn't answer.

"Uncle Anthony was too proud to call the police, but he made the servants scour the grounds. After all, how far could a little girl of seven go?"

"How far?" Jake asked in a rough rumble.

"To the beach." She saw a trickle of sweat run from his temple over the edge of his cheekbone. "There's a path," Krista continued, "that leads down the cliff. At the bottom are rock formations, some with obvious caves. I found a few that were not so obvious, and I would hide there. When I got cold or hungry, I would finally sneak back into the house—usually at night so the servants wouldn't see me. They would find me in bed in the morning. It got so they didn't bother to look after a while. They knew I'd show up eventually."

"Nobody ever tried to find out why you'd run away?"

"I wasn't any trouble, really. I always came back."

"Until now," Jake said.

"Until now."

"Forgive me." Jake's words and crease of his brow were sincere. "I didn't understand. I never imagined your reaction would be so. . .intense."

"I'm just glad. . .you didn't leave. . .that you came here."

Jake rested his forearms lightly on his knees; he closed his eyes. "Father," Jake prayed, "please help Krista to know what you want her to do with her life. Help her have the strength not to run away from the circumstances and trials you allow in her life, but to seek your strength, wisdom, and guidance. Help her to remember that she belongs to you and in Jesus Christ there is nothing too great to overcome. I ask it in Jesus' name."

"Amen." Krista's voice was very low. She studied Jake, speculation flitting across the angles of her face. He did that so easily. . .as if talking to a friend.

"Now what?" Krista asked.

"What do you want to do?"

"Right now?" Her words were slow, her face molding to a contemplative frown as she thought. "I would like to forget about all this for just a little while longer. To. . .walk and drink in the blueness of the sky and the smell of Colorado."

Straightening, Jake reached for her hand and helped Krista stand upright. "Then we'll walk," he said. His hand was warm and dry and wrapped itself securely around hers. With her free hand, she swiped at the dust and brittle pine needles clinging to her skirt, as reluctant to release herself from Jake's grip as he seemed loath to let go of her.

"There is a path," Krista suggested tentatively, "that intersects with this one and comes out on the road about a half mile down from the house."

"We'll take it. You lead the way."

The trail was steep and rocky, and Krista craved the physical exertion, the challenge of conquering the terrain, giving her the feeling that she could conquer something.

And having Jake with her, not demanding or questioning. . . .

"In case you're wondering," Krista said after some time, jumping to a level spot in the path and turning to face Jake, "I'm okay now."

"I knew you would be." His face was open, serious, but it could not hide the thoughtfulness that lingered in the depths of his darkened eyes as they continued down the hill.

—6—

Not a hint of white marred the brilliant expanse of blue, and Krista squinted against the brassy glare, adjusting her vision to the brighter surroundings as they connected with the broad main trail. A light breeze lifted the ends of her loose, damp hair, bringing some relief from the sun's steady rays.

They were just a few yards from the narrow road that snaked up the hill to the assortment of houses that lay hidden in the woods. A car crept by, carefully negotiating the curves. Krista recognized her neighbor and lifted her hand to acknowledge a waved greeting.

"Is this close to where the car almost forced you off the road last night?" Jake asked, noting the confining road. He brushed at the sweat beading on his brow and wiped his hand on his jeans.

"That was several curves back." Krista indicated the general direction of the twisted road below. "I just couldn't believe what was happening. It's a wonder I didn't go over the edge." They moved toward the side of the road to give room for any passing traffic.

"You still haven't any idea who it might have been?"

They stepped along the crumbling edge of the road, puffs of dust lifting at each movement of their feet. The grass and bushes in the ditch below were dry and layered with a thick coat of dust.

Krista shook her head, perplexity in her eyes. "I can't imagine. It all happened so fast. I didn't even think about getting a license number. I've never had anyone try to physically hurt me before."

They could hear the approach of another car, the accelerating, shifting sound muffled by a screen of trees.

"I envy you," Krista said suddenly, swiveling her head to look at Jake.

Some of the disturbance lifting from his eyes, Jake asked, "In what way?"

She tipped her squarish chin sideways and said, "I never had someone I could go to when I needed to. I envy you your family. . .and the way you pray. . .as if God's standing right beside you and all you have to do is talk to Him. You've got a relationship I don't understand—something I've only dreamed of having."

A slow smile of realization grew on Jake's face and spread to include his eyes. He turned slightly so he could concentrate on Krista.

"What I have," Jake said, "is a personal friendship with God through his Son, Jesus Christ. It's something you have, too. Two months ago you gained a whole new family."

"I know, but I find it hard. . .to pray."

"Some new Christians do. It takes time to develop a personal friendship with anyone. To re-learn thought patterns and realize there is Someone who cares all the time. With God," Jake inspected the approaching car behind them with a cursory glance, "it's no dif—"

Jake's words broke off. A spear of fright shot through Krista at the horror registering on Jake's sharpened expression.

"Wha. . ." Krista began.

Her words ended in a choking cry of pain. Jake, with a harshly snapped jerk of Krista's arm, hurled his body into hers, thrusting them off and over the crumbling edge of the road.

—7—

As a flash of dark blue roared by, they hurtled with frightening velocity into the dusty brambles of the steep ditch.

There was a skidding, gravelly, grating sound, followed by a man yelling, and a woman's shrill cry.

Krista's face was pressed into Jake's chest. She was conscious of his arm pinned under her shoulderblade, the stickiness of the bushes, the emphasized thud of Jake's heartbeat touching her ear. . .the need to breathe.

Jake stirred and spoke her name, the two syllables intense and filled with uncertainty.

He carefully shifted his crushing weight, and she drew a great, choking breath.

"Don't move," Jake ordered. "Let me see if you're all right."

She raised her hand and he snared it in his, anxiety clear in the planes of his face. His eyes, large and dark, arrested her attention as she drew huge gulps of air into her lungs.

"I. . ." She coughed at the dust and attempted to rise.

Jake pushed her back.

A man and a woman were yelling, angry, frightened voices in chorus. Car doors slammed. There was another shrill scream. . .and the man called her name.

"Krista!"

Steven?

"Steven!" Anger flared from the pit of Krista's stomach. She coughed, her eyes tightening as she glared past Jake's

shoulder to a point where her cousin and Linda were clearly outlined against the sky above them, on the road, safe.

"How could you!" Krista spat, then coughed again. She drew another breath and heaved herself past Jake's restraining hands to struggle to her feet. Then her eyes widened in horrified disbelief, and her fingers snatched at Jake. "The car! The big, *dark car. . .*"

Krista's pointed finger quavered with shock and outrage as she directed it toward Steven. "You tried to kill us!"

"Don't get hysterical," Steven drawled, his voice becoming infuriatingly calm once he realized neither Krista nor Jake were seriously injured. He slid his hands into the pockets of his white slacks. "Obviously you're still breathing."

Linda, evidently anxious to appease, her voice tense and high, inserted, "The car went out of control."

Standing next to Krista's trembling form, Jake answered, "It's no wonder, the speed you were driving."

"You did it deliberately!" Krista uttered. "*Why?*"

Krista's cousin rolled his eyes, a pucker coming to the corner of his mouth.

Linda's eyes seemed to grow and take over her pale face. Her glance darted nervously from person to person.

Speaking once more, Steven said, "It was a simple miscalculation in driving speed—nothing more."

"Was it a slight miscalculation," Krista shouted in retaliation, "when you tried to run me off the road last night?"

Steven's shoulders lifted as he gave Krista a mocking smile that slid toward Jake. "She's delirious," he said. "Once I left your establishment, I went to my hotel. Ask Linda." His gaze shifted to the anxious girl beside him. "Didn't I take you to your room and say I was going to mine?" He focused on Krista, not waiting for Linda's reply. "I even called Linda five minutes later to wish her the most pleasant of dreams." Brows rising derisively, Steven said, "If you don't believe me, that's your problem."

"I told Nan to call you off!"

Steven's dry announcement was accompanied by an indifferent shrug. "I haven't talked to Nan."

Linda clasped and unclasped her hands in spontaneous, anxiety-filled gestures—movements that irritated and provoked Krista. "We needed to see you," she added.

Krista's voice rose and her trembling advanced to violent shaking. "You've seen me," she said, "now *go away!*"

Jake snatched Krista closer to himself, protecting her in the hard embrace of his arms. She buried her face in his shirt, in the dirt and sweat and deep echoing sound of his voice coming from the depth of his chest.

"Whatever you need," Jake said evenly, "make it quick, because I'm taking Krista home."

Krista tightened her grip around Jake's waist, as she twisted her head to see her cousin and his girlfriend. Steven appeared unaffected.

"I have something for Krista," Steven said, flashing a look at Linda. The girl turned and scurried away. "It was to have been delivered last night, but I obviously didn't have the opportunity to do that."

"Whatever it is, I don't want it!" Krista snapped.

Linda dashed back with a manila envelope that she thrust at Steven. He held it up and waited, then realized with rueful resignation that neither Krista nor Jake were about to ascend the embankment to obtain the packet.

With a twist of his lips and a sigh, Steven Mariano stepped, skidding in the dirt and weeds, down the side of the ditch, gathering a film of light brown dust on the tailored slacks and soft leather shoes. He regarded the damage distastefully and, handing the envelope to Jake when Krista refused to take it, he offered with an air of bored courtesy, "Might I give you a lift home?"

"*No!*"

Jake's hand was on Krista's, enfolding it in a reassuring squeeze. "We'll manage on our own," he replied.

Squeezing her eyes tightly shut, Krista waited. She heard Steven scrambling up the way he had come, Linda's soft murmur, Steven's reply.

Two doors slammed, and Steven's car roared to life, spitting gravel as it turned and sped toward the city.

—8—

A strange silence enveloped them as Jake opened the front door to Krista's house.

Krista sank wearily onto the light-colored sofa next to Jake, unmindful of the dirt that clung to their clothes. Placing her palms flat on the knobby surface of the furniture, she pulled them forward and backward until the irritation caused her to ball her fists and lay them in her lap. She tilted her head against the back of the sofa.

"I hate him!" Her whispered words spit themselves out of her mouth before she could stop them. "I hate all of them, Jake. I know I shouldn't, but I can't help how I feel. I feel so... inadequate to deal with them." She turned and pierced Jake's look with her own. "I used to be stronger. I've grown weak. I never used to. . .lose control like this."

Jake's sympathy softened his features. He plucked a tiny twig from a lock of hair that stuck to the side of her cheek and brushed the damp strands back. "I know it's hard. And I know you're scared. I am, too. But God is over all this and there's a purpose behind these happenings. You'll see. This will work out for the best."

Unable to sit, Jake got up, prowling from window to window, glancing at the view, studying the surrounding countryside. Krista followed him with her eyes, knowing his inward attempt to broach the issue at hand, to have his questions answered. She half wished he would ask. . .and half wished he would not.

Krista studied her hands and the streaks of dirt that

covered the tiny scratches on her arms. Her legs had not survived unscathed, either, and were beginning to itch. Absently, she rubbed a hand down the back of one calf.

How could her display of temper and lack of self-control not alienate her from Jake? And yet, he was here. He had not condemned her flight through the woods or her barrage of words when she spoke against Steven and her uncle and Nan.

"I'm sorry," Krista said very quietly, "that you got involved in my family troubles."

"I'm not," he countered, stopping his restless movements. He turned and faced her squarely, raising the envelope Steven had given him. "But since I am involved," one eyebrow lifted, "I would like to know what I'm up against. What is this?"

"I don't know," she answered truthfully. "Although I do have a good idea."

A slight frown creased his face. "Don't you think it's important enough to open?"

"Yes."

"But you won't."

"I can't!" Her hands snapped outward in a wide, unexpected gesture. She stopped. That was not how she wanted to be. *Dear God, help me.* Her eyes focused on the envelope that would take her one step closer to doing what Uncle Anthony planned.

When would it stop? Could she delude herself into believing it would?

Krista fought the tense, tear-filled feeling that threatened to overwhelm her. Her jaw set and her lips thinned in defense.

The furrow grew deeper between Jake's brows and the silence lengthened between them. Krista had no armor against his direct, disconcerting gaze, so she averted her eyes to study her hands again.

A bird gave a sharp cry outside the window, scolding the

squirrels that stole from its feeder. The clock on the wall chimed the hour. It was later than Krista had thought.

Jake shifted his stance. The envelope crackled between his fingers. "Seeing as how this envelope nearly cost both of us our lives, I'd say it's important enough to know what's inside."

Blinking her eyes slowly, she tipped her chin his direction. He was right. She knew he was right.

Moving forward several steps, Jake flicked his wrist. The envelope slapped on the glass-topped table and slid a couple of inches toward her.

Jake eased himself onto the edge of the sofa. He lifted her fists carefully and slid his thumbs into her palms to uncurl her fingers.

"I'm sorry. You didn't deserve that from me. I'm tired," Jake admitted. "I'm worried. I don't understand what's going on. I'd like to be able to take all your trials and hurl them over the farthest mountain, but I can't do that. I just want you to know," his fingers tightened on hers, "that I am here whenever you need me. That I care about you very much. That I will do everything I can to protect you and keep you safe." He paused, adding, "I will be satisfied," the somber depth of his green eyes sought hers, "with the information you've given me."

"And. . .you won't be offended if I ask you to go home?"

"If that's what you want, I'll go." His face stiffened the tiniest bit. "Are you sure you'll be safe? Steven. . ."

Her head shook slightly. "If you're worried about Steven returning, I don't think you need be. In spite of what I accused him of, I really doubt that he intentionally tried to run us down. I was upset and wanted someone to blame for last night. Last night it was dark. Everything happened so quickly. The car could have been any color. Quite frankly, I don't think he could purposely do something like that.

"Steven's accomplished what he was sent to do, and he's prone to self-indulgence. He won't bother himself with anything more than he has to. Believe me," she said when more than a touch of doubt tightened the corners of Jake's eyes. "I know my cousin. He won't be back. Also, I know you need to be at McIntyres'. The meat shipment arrives today." Her head shook with a slight motion. "When are you going to get any sleep?"

Jake laughed outright, a surprisingly pleasing sound. "I thought I was the one who was going to worry about you and here you are arranging my day for me." He sobered quickly. "Okay, I'll go, if that's what you want—if you feel that certain about Steven. But if you need me, you know where to find me."

Krista squeezed his fingers and released herself from his grip. Rising, she waited for Jake to follow her initiative.

"I'll call later," Jake offered.

"Thanks. I'll plug in the phone. . .later."

Jake's hand touched Krista's shoulder. She gazed upward toward his face.

"I'll be praying for you." Jake's words hung in the air. The intensity of his expression echoed the sincerity of his words.

"I'd like that."

Jake smiled, a smile that accompanied a vaguely disturbed expression that settled in the vicinity of his eyes.

His hand came away from her shoulder and he was gone.

—9—

Krista moved the palms of her hands across the fabric of her skirt and stared at the door. She heard Jake's car door close, the start of his engine, and the crunch of gravel as he drove away toward the city.

Exhaling a weary breath, Krista rubbed her face with her hands and pushed her hair back from her cheeks.

What a difference a matter of hours could bring.

She glanced around the room, turning to see the home she had made away from Anthony Mariano's millions. Away from the Mariano influence. She wanted to deny that Uncle Anthony had found her. . .but it wasn't possible.

Krista sank into a corner of the sofa and hugged a throw pillow of the same creamy, knobby texture. Her line of vision wandered. She saw, hanging on the wall, the muted, yet bold, pastel print she bought just because it was splashy and she liked the colors. On the bookcase arranged with her books stood a carved apple-faced doll she purchased because it caught her eye. There were a dozen items, large and small, she had used to make her home her own personal, private place.

No expensive paintings, no collector items. No sixteenth century furniture or elegant marble.

The envelope was a reach away.

Krista licked her lips and the weight on her chest grew to a tremendous pressure.

She shoved the pillow away. Trembling fingers plucked the envelope from off the glass.

Krista pulled the tabs and slid her fingertip under the flap, tipping the envelope to allow the contents to slip out.

A sheet of heavy, cream colored stationery fell into her hand. . .along with a folder containing a plane ticket.

The papers quivered between her fingers.

A scrolled, golden "M" laced the upper corner of the stationery, and below was a letter written in a forcefully masculine scrawl that was somehow crooked, bent at the edges. Anthony Mariano's authority, Krista's lips twisted, was being undermined by an ancient enemy: Age.

My Dear Krista,

The passiveness of those simple words caused her stomach to churn.

It has taken many months for us to find you. Why you are where you are I cannot imagine, save to say that you chose someplace you thought undiscoverable. Yet, I doubt there is anyone I am not capable of finding, given the sport to do so.

I have endured much concern for your well-being in these past many months. I trust that by now you have seen the purpose behind what I have done for you. After all, you are a Mariano, and it is of the utmost importance for you to uphold the family name with discretion—something which, obviously, Steven has no compulsion to do.

Typical of him to insert that jab. He never missed a chance. . .even if it was true.

My plans lie in you. Enclosed is a plane ticket for your arrival home. You have simply to contact Nan, and she will arrange for you to be met at the airport.

Please do what you know is right.

The letter was signed with a flourish.

Krista's lips thinned. Angry shadows crossed her face. Inwardly she rebelled against the reflex to placate her

49

uncle's demands. . .as subtle as they might be. Even as she shredded the stiff paper between her fingers, she abhorred herself, her weakness toward the dictates of her uncle.

Krista shook her head, running her hands across her face, rubbing circulation into her stiff features.

She needed a shower.

She needed some sleep.

She needed to go to McIntyres'.

—10—

Krista entered her parking slot at the restaurant. Jake's car was there, along with Darrell's and a few others.

Krista had, through sheer exhaustion, managed to obtain an hour of mercifully dreamless sleep. When she awakened, her decision was firmly set in her mind, and she lost no time in putting her plan into action.

Soft, rolling, musical chords greeted her ears when she unlocked and relocked the front door. Hearing the piano produced a vague calming, and she knew she was right to have come here. No matter what the next days would bring, she would have McIntyres' to remember.

Krista strode the carpeted hall to the vacated eating area where Darrell sat at his piano. One of his hands trickled the melody of a piece while the other held the score.

Darrell glanced at Krista from the corner of his eye and mentioned, "Jake's catching a few minutes' sleep in his office." The chords hung in the air as he continued his playing. "I heard you weren't feeling well last night."

"Only a headache," Krista answered, weaving her way through the tables and up the two curved steps to stand next to the piano. She slipped her hands into the deep, slash pockets of her cotton sundress. "That sounds nice."

"It's a beautiful piece," Darrell agreed. He settled the score on the ledge and put both hands to the keys. Music floated around them, filling the room with a hauntingly lovely melody.

Darrell looked at her and winked, a friendly, encompassing

51

expression that swelled a bittersweet emotion in her breast.

Krista asked, "Will you be playing it tonight?"

A noncommittal drawl came from Darrell. He stopped and backtracked, playing a succession of notes twice before continuing. "It needs practice. Maybe by the weekend." A smile flashed her way. "I'll play it especially for you then." His hands stopped and he regarded her seriously. "I heard you and Jake had a close call this morning. Jake mentioned something, too, about a car trying to run you off the road last night. Is that true?"

Krista shrugged, a look of doubt shadowing her eyes. "I don't know. At the time I was sure the car had tried to run me off the road. But it could have been a reckless driver." Krista's brow wrinkled. "Who would want to do that to me?" She did not wait for an answer. "But as far as my cousin is concerned, Steven has a complete lack of consideration for anyone other than himself. We were fortunate we weren't really hurt." As Darrell paused, she added, "Don't quit. I enjoy hearing you play."

"If you say so." Darrell began a series of running melodies that had nothing to do with the notes on the musical score in front of him. An eyebrow rose in her direction. "Jake's worried about you."

Studying Darrell's hands moving across the keys, she answered, "I know."

"You're pretty special to him."

Krista raised her line of her vision from Darrell's hands to meet his gaze. "I don't know why." Her voice was soft, but serious.

The fair-colored brow remained aloft and Darrell's hands halted. After a moment the brow shifted to its normal position and he resumed playing. "Does it matter why?"

"It might."

Darrell's lips pursed and he glanced to a point somewhere

across the room before turning back to Krista. "I'll tell you something you may or may not know. Jake's been interested in you since the first day you interviewed for a job here at McIntyres'. Since you became a Christian, that interest has doubled with a seriousness I've never seen before in my brother. If you're concerned about the fact that you're a Mariano—yes, he told me," Darrell inserted as her surprise registered, "don't give it a second thought. Jake is not a gold digger."

"Why are you telling me this, Darrell?"

He shrugged. "We both know you've been keeping Jake at arm's length. I wonder now, if it's because you're a Mariano. Or," he made a movement with his shoulder, "perhaps there's an entirely different reason. Only you know why." Darrell twitched his lips as he considered his thoughts. "We've both been concerned, Jake and I, but he won't push you. Me? Maybe I'm a bit more forward." He smiled a moderately contrite apology. "Whatever it is that's hindering you, Jake'll wait it out. You can trust him."

The music stopped. Darrell said, "Jake cares."

"I know. But I can't get involved. Not now. Not yet."

Studying Krista for a moment, Darrell replied, "You know best for yourself, I suppose."

—11—

Jake's office door was open about an inch, so Krista peeked through the crack, giving the door a nudge to widen the opening. Jake appeared to be asleep still. His long legs dangled over the end of the loveseat and an extra pillow was caught in his arms. He had not changed his clothes or showered.

Krista debated on whether or not to disturb him. She knew he had a long night ahead of him, and her own hour of sleep had come too dearly.

However, her indecision was taken from her when Jake shifted, gave a soft groan, and contorted his features. He reached to knead the muscles at the back of his neck.

Krista spoke, pushing the door open further. "If you plan to sleep here," one of Jake's eyes opened to a narrow slit, "you should invest in a larger sofa."

"Not enough room," he grumbled, throwing his legs to the floor so he could sit upright. "How come you aren't home getting some sleep yourself?" His eyes widened. "Has something else happened?"

Krista met his eyes squarely. "No—not in the way you might think."

Gesturing for her to come in, Jake shoved the pillow to one side so he could perch on the edge of the couch.

"So," he said. "Tell me what I might not think."

Tightening her fingers into fists inside the dress pockets, Krista lifted her chin the merest fraction. "I'm leaving," she said. "I just stopped to let you know."

Bewildered surprise gathered in Jake's eyes and his lips parted slightly as his jaw grew slack.

"I'm going to California," Krista continued. "Today. I'm packed and ready to leave, and I just stopped to let you know. I apologize for not giving more advance notice, but. . . ."

Jake brushed aside her words with an abrupt wave of his hand as he stood. A frown was overcoming his initial reaction. "That was a sudden decision," he said.

"But not impetuous."

Krista took three steps across the homey, cluttered office before turning to face him once more. Giving him a direct stare, she leaned back against the desk, bracing her hands on either side of the desktop for support.

"I am choosing to do this. . .not because Uncle Anthony has demanded it of me," her head shook decisively, "but because I have to face what's there. I'm doing it my way, however. My terms, my decision. I'm standing my ground, Jake. I have to make it clear to him that I won't run anymore. I won't be manipulated according to his will." She drew in a slow breath. Her brave words did not completely quell her uneasiness. "The only way for him to realize that," she went on, "is to tell him to his face. . .and leave with him watching me walk out the door."

Jake's frown deepened to a perplexed scowl. The gesture of his hand emphasized his pointed words. "I can't say I like your choice. From what I've seen, I get the distinct impression you're jumping headlong into trouble."

"I am," Krista admitted candidly. "Yet, I have to do this. Uncle Anthony faces only cold, hard facts. That's why he's the excellent businessman he is. . .as were his father and his father's father before him." She paused. "I am scared, Jake. Resolved, but frightened. I shouldn't ask, but. . .I need your support in a very special way."

"I can be ready in an hour," he said. "Just give me time to settle a few things. . . ."

"No." Krista shook her head and laid a restraining hand on his arm as she tried to draw her thoughts into spoken words. "Thank you, but I'm going alone." She stopped. "I don't want to sound melodramatic, and I feel as if I'm asking an awful lot of you. . . but," she hesitated, unsure now of how foolish she might sound.

Jake watched her. "Go on."

"I want. . .to make sure I come home. To Colorado. I'm not certain what might happen, but. . .I. . .need—would like—your support."

A puzzled frown creased his face. "How can I ensure that if I'm not with you?"

Krista fumbled a slip of paper from her dress pocket. "This is the estate number," she said, "and my personal number. . .as long as it hasn't been changed, and I see no reason for it to have been changed." Jake took the paper without looking at it, and Krista avoided his grim study. "Call me. Often." Her hands were shaking and Jake grasped them with his own, the paper crackling between their clasped fingers.

Jake's voice was husky, his eyes filled with a deep, entreating earnestness. "What was in that envelope?"

Hurt shadowed Krista's face. "A letter. . .and a plane ticket."

"You're flying?"

"The ticket is confetti in my garbage. It was one way, not round trip."

"He really expected you not to return here?" Perplexed astonishment swept across Jake's fair features. "What sort of man is he?"

"He is. . .Anthony Mariano."

The telephone rang, a muted, yet jarring noise, and Jake glanced at it in minor irritation. After three rings someone answered it, but the light showed the conversation on that line.

Jake's sigh was one of resignation as he said, "You're leaving today."

"My car is packed, the house is shut. I'll leave from here."

"How long will you be gone?"

"I would like," she said, disengaging her hands from Jake's and sliding her fingers into her pockets, "to be gone no longer than a week—if possible."

Jake ran a hand across his mouth and started to speak, but was stopped by a light tap on the open door.

Darrell, eyebrows risen and stature slightly inclined as he leaned around the door, said, "There's a phone call for Krista, line one."

Jake, glancing at Krista then back to Darrell, asked, "Did the person give a name?"

"It was a woman. She said her name was Nan Carr and that it was absolutely imperative she talk with Krista."

Jake's concerned look flicked over Krista's tightened features.

Setting her jaw, Krista lifted her chin and resolutely reached for the telephone.

"Krista. . ." The older woman's voice was the same as earlier—soft, determined, matter-of-fact. "I regret to have to tell you this. Please brace yourself since it cannot be put any other way." Nan paused.

Dread seeped into the pit of Krista's stomach, and she unconsciously rubbed the palm of her hand against her midsection.

"Your Uncle Anthony," Nan continued, "died an hour ago in his sleep. It was. . .unexpected. He had improved this past week. We thought. . .he was getting better." There was a minute pause. "They will be taking him away soon. As mistress of Mariano Estate, what do you want me to do?"

Silence crackled over the line. Krista's stomach churned.

She swallowed and swayed against the desk, allowing its weight to support her own.

"Krista," Nan's voice asked, "are you still there?"

Krista gripped the receiver tighter, her fingers numb, cold. "He was that ill?" she managed.

"I asked you to come home."

"I. . .had decided to." Krista ran her fingertips along her brow and down to her lips. *Dead?* Nausea threatened. "But," she continued, "there wasn't enough time, I guess." Her words were a mere whisper.

"The funeral arrangements," Nan was saying, "have all been taken care of, so you need not be concerned about that. We need you home, however. Quince can meet your arrival on the next flight."

The next flight. . .

Krista licked her lips and attempted to swallow. Her look flickered to Jake who had stretched a strong arm about her shoulders. "I. . ." Her voice was raspy and strange. "I. . .will be there in time for the funeral. Don't send Quince to the airport. I don't intend to fly."

"Honestly, Krista. . .I realize this is not pleasant, but you should be here to supervise arrangements."

"Uncle Anthony was not one to be unprepared." Krista's lips twisted in a grimace. "Even for his own death. You can handle what needs to be done. I'm driving. I'll be leaving in the next few minutes. I. . .I'll be there in two or three days."

—12—

Krista had not packed much. All her personal things would still be in her rooms, she knew—as if she had never driven away two years before.

When she fled California, she had taken very little. Her mother and father had left their only daughter with more than enough to live comfortably without her Uncle Anthony's millions. She assumed that, somehow through her lawyer, Anthony Mariano had discovered her whereabouts.

Not that any of that mattered now. Uncle Anthony was. . . gone.

Traveling beyond the Rocky Mountains, Krista crossed heated deserts and salt flats to more mountains and through the valleys of northern California. Twice she thought she saw the same black car that had nearly run her off the road but dismissed the idea as paranoia.

However, her tenseness grew as each mile brought increasingly familiar sights. The northern coast was an arresting picture of towering cliffs and pounding surf or gently sloping beaches. And the redwoods. . .tall, magnificent, stately in the clinging, misty, late evening, summer fog.

She wished she were in Colorado.

Exiting the highway, Krista turned and wove through the small, coastal town she had once called home. Tourism was important for the town's people, and having the estate of Anthony Mariano here was not a detriment to business.

Krista slowed and downshifted, fingers whitening as she clutched the leather-wrapped steering wheel. Her car swung obediently along the high, narrow street that followed the curve of the bay.

Directly across the calm stretch of water lay a finger of land thrust protectively between the ocean and town. Mariano Estate was there—reigning high on the ocean bluff, surrounded by wind-sculptured cedars bent permanently away from the ocean forces. The house, angling slightly townward on the peculiarly-set, pointing twist of land, towered white, two and a half stories high, with wings at forty-five degree angles off either end.

Golden-red rectangles flashed in the evening sunset from the tall, wide windows. The house was graceful of line, reminiscent of southern architecture, built five generations prior to Krista.

Krista ran her sweaty palms, each in turn, down her denim-clad legs. She continued the winding ascent up the backside of the bluff, the blazing, golden-red of the sun gone as suddenly as it appeared, replaced once more by the damp curls of fog that transformed the dramatically fragile coastal beauty to swirling grey.

The grounds were encircled by eight foot, wrought iron fencing, and the gate was attended by a man whom she did not recognize.

Krista rolled down her window.

The man stooped to take a look at Krista's face and gave a brief smile. "Miss Johnston. . .please drive on. You are expected."

The gate slid back electronically, permitting her access to the grounds. Lifting her hand in reply to the man's gesture, Krista put her little car in gear and eased up the rock driveway, stopping before she reached the front door.

She had not expected people. At least not this many.

Expensive cars of every color lined the drive. Even with the damp cold, small groups of people stood around talking.

Krista's presence did not go undetected as she maneuvered

her car along the curving drive past the front of the house with its wide, graceful steps and columns. However, there was more curiosity than recognition on the part of the people who witnessed her arrival. There to pay homage to the late Anthony Mariano, they did not realize that the new heiress to the great fortune had driven past in a late model sports car, wearing blue jeans and a plain silk blouse.

Beyond the far wing stood the garages and, as if by magic, the third door from the right, where she used to park, began to raise. Evidently the house had been alerted to her arrival.

Krista turned into the building and parked, twisting the key in the ignition to the off position. Her body hummed from the miles of travel—a sort of buzz that took over her sense of feeling. She gripped the steering wheel tightly and dropped her forehead onto the back of her hands.

She was here. . .Mariano Estate.

A small disturbance caught her attention, and Krista lifted her eyes to see one of the old servants, this time a familiar face, standing discreetly some distance away in the cavernous excuse for a garage. A silent apology crossed the man's features as he awaited her exit from her car.

Cracking her car door open, Krista eased it back several inches. Cold, damp air leaked into the car.

Krista spoke. "I haven't much, Dean. I'll take my own things in."

"Begging your pardon, Miss Johnston," the man replied, taking one respectful step forward. "Miss Carr instructed me to clean your vehicle once you arrived."

"You know I prefer to take care of my own belongings. I'll assume full responsibility for any repercussions from Miss Carr."

The man gave a brief smile along with a slight bow and exited quietly.

Krista permitted the car door to close, but not latch, as she took note of the old man's progress past the covered mounds that were the cream Rolls Royce and the mint '54 Chevy. The slit of grey daylight beyond the doorway blinked off as the servant passed through and the door closed.

First confrontation down. . .but the gnawing uneasiness she had endured since first seeing Steven at McIntyres' grew in intensity.

Krista's glance flicked toward a moving shadow as her heart gave an erratic thump. Her hand touched her throat. A cat moved. She was jittery, she admitted to herself.

Krista began to gather her things, shoving garbage into a small brown bag. She pulled her roomy, denim jacket out from behind the passenger seat and struggled to slip her arms into the sleeves, giving the zipper a deliberate thrust upward to her throat.

Rounded rock from the path slipped beneath her shoes, the smooth surfaces forcing themselves into the thin soles of her leather flats. Krista shivered, pulling her ladened arms closer to herself. No matter. She had any number of sweaters and light wool jackets in her room. . .more than enough for the time she would be here.

The handful of people she passed not far from the garage conspicuously curtailed all conversation while she was within listening range. It was obvious they were curious about this plainly dressed girl who parked her car with Anthony Mariano's private car collection.

Intentionally ducking her head, Krista altered her foot-steps, taking a sudden sharp turn and ignoring the path to the main entrance. She swung around the wing of the house to the gymnasium on the off chance those doors would be unlocked. By using the back hallway she could make it to her rooms virtually undisturbed.

Having always been mildly reclusive himself unless business dictated otherwise, Uncle Anthony had never demanded that Krista be in the limelight. She was grateful, in whatever small way she could be grateful to her uncle, for that. Few people knew she was heiress to the Mariano fortune.

The heavy gymnasium door swung toward her even as she began to shift the articles she carried.

Nan. Of course.

"I thought perhaps you might try this entrance." Mariano Estate's housekeeper was saying. Her soft voice echoed against the far-flung walls and girdered ceiling. The door whispered shut with a click, the sound repeating itself in the shadowed emptiness of the vast room.

Nan was the same as Krista remembered—petite, immaculate, with a trace of lavender teasing Krista's nostrils as to whether it was really there. Perhaps there were a few strands more of silver threaded throughout Nan's knotted, dark hair. Her eyes were sunken, reddened as if by weeping. However, the housekeeper's face was composed and orderly—her commitment to duty intact.

"You must be tired after such a long trip," Nan's hands were outstretched, willing to be of help with Krista's burdens.

Krista ignored Nan's silent offer. "How many more people will be coming?"

"These are our guests, friends of your uncle's, from out of town, many of them," Nan said. "Of course we should open the house to them."

"Of course," Krista parroted flatly.

"Once you've rested a bit you must take the time to accept their condolences," Nan continued, speaking low as she trailed Krista across the polished, wooden floors.

Krista shoved past the inside gymnasium doors and entered the hall where a wide staircase led up to the wing of bedrooms. Ignoring the staircase, Krista turned to pass through another doorway, hidden far back under the stairs.

Her thin leather shoes whispered preternaturally loud in

the shadowed, narrow back hall. Nan's footsteps were an imitation of her own. The skin crawled on the back of Krista's neck. When she reached another stairway ascending on her right, she quickly turned, her feet giving soft, staccato taps as she hurried up the steps.

Nan's voice carried along the stairwell. "I will bring some refreshment to you shortly."

Stopping with one foot resting on the step above her, she turned to face Nan. "Do not reprimand Dean for not cleaning my car. I told him not to."

Krista went through the door at the landing, hesitating briefly in the tiny alcove where a single window gave a view of the tops of the cedars and the sea beyond.

Turning her back, Krista continued along the wide hall, her footsteps muffled by thick, wine colored carpet. Farther down the hall on her right was Steven's suite. Also, the group of rooms Linda must be using. Both doors were closed, which was just as well. She had no desire to talk to either of them.

The first door on her left—the one to her living quarters— was open and, a sense of despondency washing over her, Krista halted, just inside the room.

Her suite had not changed.

She leaned on the door, pushing it shut against the memories that had enveloped her since she entered the house.

Before her was the sitting room, appealing in Queen Anne decor with its delicate curves and ageless beauty and marbled fireplace. The pink and silver decorating carried over to the personal dining room that lay through the archway directly ahead. Beyond the linen covered table were French doors that led to the balcony overlooking the ballroom. To Krista's left was the bedroom, with the cherrywood four-poster bed, her desk, a mirrored dresser. . .with her perfumes and brushes, even a necklace remained on top, as if she had never left.

An eerie quiver crept down Krista's back. She laid her things, along with her jacket, on the mauve-covered bed and strode silently to the pair of tall, double windows. Through them she could see the identical view she had encountered in the hallway: the ocean. . .its grey-black color cold and foreboding.

Krista exhaled and passed her hands over her eyes, raking her nails up through her hair, giving a firm tug on its straight length. Surviving this evening, the next day, and the time she would be here was all she asked—to mentally and physically retain her self control, her. . .self-respect.

A brief prayer wandered through her mind. *Lord, I'm not strong enough for this. Protect me. Help me.*

Her thoughts flitted to Jake. He was different from anyone else she knew. Krista's brow puckered. What did being a Christian really mean to her? She had accepted Jesus Christ as her Savior that night at church with Jake. But what made the difference in Jake's family's life? In his life?

She ached suddenly for his congenial face. . .and his wish to be her buffer against the strain of who she was. Or—she considered thoughtfully—who she was forced to be.

But, she had left Jake in Colorado.

The faint clink of silver drew Krista back to reality. She knew, without investigation, that Nan had entered, and that the table in her dining room was being properly prepared to serve a company of one.

Krista continued to study the darkened sky, turning only when a faint whisper of sound alerted her to Nan's presence in her bedroom.

"You may leave my jacket where it is," Krista ordered in a strained voice as Nan whisked it from where it lay on the bed.

"Nonsense," Nan replied, grasping the article by its shoulders and giving it a shake. The orange Krista had placed in the pocket struck the carpeted floor with a muffled thud. Nan bent, grasped the object with her fingers and, with no hesitation, dropped the offensive fruit in the pocket of her apron.

Krista suppressed the overwhelming urge to retaliate against Nan for that seemingly innocent gesture. Nan had usually discounted whatever Krista had said or done.

"I am certain," Nan's attention returned to Krista's jacket, "you do not want it wrinkled. It is just right," the housekeeper's gaze swept over Krista's travel rumpled attire, "for your casual wear."

Nan flicked open the closet door, turned on the light and entered the small room to extract a hanger.

Finding her tongue, Krista countered, "Of course, you were always there to counsel my indecisions." She added, "I like what I am wearing."

"It will never do for this evening." Hangers clicked. Nan considered various selections, pushing aside pale silks in favor of navys and blacks.

"What I have on," Krista said, "will do fine for this evening since I do not plan to attend any social functions."

"But. . ." Nan's searching ceased, "all these people are here to offer their sympathy for your loss."

"They are here to sight see and scrutinize the presumed heiress of Anthony Mariano's millions. . .and I will not be a puppet on parade."

The light went out. The closet door closed.

Nan began patiently, her hands in front of her, one folded over the top of the other, "Your Uncle Anthony. . ."

". . .Is dead, Nan. Dead. I don't need to know what he would think, because I know already." She gave a disappointed exclamation, her hands cartwheeling through the air. "Don't you think that after twenty-one years under his constant

66

tutelage I should know what he would consider were my responsibilities?"

Nan's lips thinned. "I will. . .inform our guests that you are too weary from your travels to make an appearance."

"Now or at any other time."

Nan's mouth came open in protest.

"Don't give them the impression," Krista's tone took on a threatening quality, "that I will be on display at any other time, Nan. I won't show."

"The funeral. . ."

"That," Krista conceded, "is the one time I will make a public appearance. But I will not have it a farcical free-for-all."

Nan's eyes widened. "These people. . ."

". . .Are old acquaintances—friends, if you so desire to call them such—of my uncle. I neither know them nor care to know them."

"Admiral Epstein is here. . .and Mr. and Mrs. Farlow. Their daughter, Jennifer, has been asking to see you. And there are the Trendens and Cedargates. . . ."

"No one," Krista reiterated emphatically.

Nan's folded grip moved with the barest of tremors.

Holding her hand out to Nan, Krista spoke, "I'll take my orange back now."

There was the slightest of hesitancy. Nan's fingers loosened their grasp from themselves. One hand slipped into her large apron pocket to remove the rounded fruit. It glowed a dull orange-yellow, a direct incongruity to the pinks and silvers around them.

"Ring," Nan's voice returned to the measured cadence of a servant, "if you need anything. I will come whenever you call."

Krista observed Nan's straight back, the even, quiet steps of Mariano Estate's housekeeper, as the woman walked to the door. Nan paused, turning to Krista.

Krista silently withstood the scrutiny of the woman who

67

had been her companion from the day she entered the Mariano Estate household at the age of three.

Nan's voice was quiet when she spoke. "Do think about your position and who you are, Krista. Don't snub these people. They are very important to you and your future."

"My future does not lie with these people. Also, I will want my automatic openers for the garage and front gate. I prefer not being hindered coming or going. . .or having my movements monitored."

The tense words hung in the air between the two women. Nan gave a short nod of her head and exited, pulling the door closed behind her.

Releasing a shaky breath, Krista spun about. She ran her hands over her face, drawing a breath through her fingers. Her eyes closed, then reopened.

Small victories, Krista thought to herself, can taste very bitter. She shook her head. It was not what she wanted, to act this way, but she knew Nan would not respect what she said otherwise. To Nan she was still a small child to be manipulated into submission.

Rotating her shoulders backward to loosen the tightened muscles, Krista made her way through the sitting room to the covered French doors. The door opened easily, and she slipped onto the sheltered balcony, permitting the draperies to fall back and hide the light behind them. The curved space was small, shadowed, and designed to be intimate. It was perfect for observing the panorama below.

The distinct hum of voices lifted easily to her, intensified rather than diminished by the great size of the ballroom. Men and women milled about the polished floor, clustering in conversational groups or consuming tidbits from the countless offerings on the buffet tables. Jewels glistened and dresses sparkled in the light of the extravagant chandeliers that illuminated the room.

Krista could only guess at the number in attendance. How

many others would arrive by tomorrow? The less wealthy, but no less influential. Or those high-ranking personnel from any number of the various firms and businesses he owned.

Krista twisted her lips. Anthony Mariano had a knack for instilling loyalty to himself—not all of it due to his wealth.

Hugging her arms to herself, Krista considered that same essence of loyalty had been ingrained in her, tempered with the underlying, silent dictate that she was to do exactly as she was instructed.

For twenty-one of her twenty-six years she had.

A sudden chill touched Krista. The distinct impression she was being watched caused her to survey again the shifting groups of people below. Yet, no upturned face appeared to be watching her balcony.

Not satisfied with what she saw, Krista's line of vision shifted right and left and finally across the space of the ballroom to where another long row of protected balconies extended from guest rooms.

Who could be watching her? In the shadows, as she was, it would be difficult for anyone to know she was there—unless they had seen the light as she entered the balcony.

Puzzled, Krista searched again, opposite her balcony and to the right of another balcony across the room.

At that moment a figure drew itself out of the protective shadows to lean, intimidatingly, on the railing.

—13—

Krista gasped sharply and stepped back.

The shoulders were as wide, the arms as thick, straining, she could see even at this distance, the cut of the dark evening jacket. The hair was as deep in color. . . the tilt of the head the same.

Thrusting herself past the draperies into her suite, Krista jerked the glass door closed. The drapes shuddered with her passing and became still.

Broderick? Here? Now?

What was she going to do?

Tremulous hands flew to her ashen cheeks. She gave a thin shriek when the suite door flew inward.

Steven, brows raised in amused observation, urged Linda through the open doorway.

"It would be nice if you knocked," Krista stated in a flare of exasperation.

"We're family," Steven replied with an airy shrug of his shoulders.

Giving the door a shove to insure privacy for their conversation, Krista demanded, "What is Broderick doing here?"

Genuine surprise registered on her cousin's face, then he grinned pleasantly. "Perhaps he's decided you're fair game again. . .now that Uncle Anthony is gone."

"And what do you want?" she asked.

Steven smiled. "To show off Linda."

Lifting his companion's hand, Steven puckered his lips as

if to blow a kiss and twirled Linda in the middle of the room, her hair and skirt flowing in a graceful arc. "Isn't she ravishing?"

Krista noted the expensive cut of the shimmering gown and the glitter of diamonds encircling Linda's throat. Pity overcame her for Linda's sake. The girl obviously adored Steven and was naive enough to trust him.

"Nice," she conceded to Linda, a semblance of civility claiming her tongue before she returned her attention to Steven. "You must have won a sizeable bet."

Her cousin shrugged. "Not bad."

"It's regrettable you haven't learned that gambling doesn't pay—especially when it's not your own money."

Shrugging off her comment, Steven said, "It's my night for introducing Linda to Uncle Anthony's business associates. . . and various other acquaintances." Casting a glance at Krista's attire, he added, "You're not coming down?"

"No."

"You always were prudish about the fun things in life."

Krista shot Steven a sharp look. "That depends on what you see as being fun."

"Fun to you is a common waitressing job."

"It's better than gambling Uncle Anthony's fortune away."

"Don't like me spending your money, Krista? I already know what Uncle Anthony thought of my business capacity. I'm not so stupid as to think he'd leave the greater portion to me. Although," Steven's eyes gleamed as he enunciated each syllable of his next words as if with a subtle caress, "there are always. . .possibilities. By the way," he inserted before Krista could reply, "where is your Mr. McIntyre? I half expected him to accompany you."

"I asked him not to come."

Steven's brows lifted with a sudden, "Oh ho! And you

thought you'd throw me off by demanding to know what Broderick was doing here. I see; you wanted no interference."

Disgusted, Krista said, "You would think that way."

A tight smile settled on Steven's features. "If I see Broderick, I'll let him know you're asking about him."

"It's time for you to leave," Krista stated. "I'll handle Broderick my way."

As soon as the door closed behind the retreating couple, Krista turned and scurried to the chest of drawers in her bedroom to riffle through a pile of sweaters. The short time Steven and Linda had been in her room had given her a moment to think. She extracted a creamy cable pullover that she knew was warm. Pulling it over her head, she snatched her jacket off its hanger and hurried out.

There was no one in the hall. Rushing down the narrow back stairs, Krista located the seldom used exit door off the lower hall and fiddled with the lock until it snapped back. She burst into the damp night.

Chill air lifted strands of hair about her face and tickled the back of her neck. Krista flipped up the collar of her jacket and tucked her chin behind the top of the zipper. She hunched her shoulders and crossed the grounds to where the cliff broke away to meet the ocean.

Ignoring the flagstone path, she cut directly across the yard until she came to the fencing that guarded the cliff. Krista hurried along it until she reached the gate that blocked the descending, twisting walkway used to reach the bayward side of the beach front that bordered Mariano Estate.

If it really was Broderick she had seen, he would not take long before he came to find her. He would have seen her re-enter her rooms when the draperies were pulled back.

The heavy gate was slick and cold beneath her hands, but it slid silently open and shut. Krista dropped the latch to secure it into place and began her careful descent. Thankfully, the fog was lifting. A few scattered stars and the uncertain shine of the moon lent some direction to her feet, besides the shadowed footlights placed at intervals along the path.

Touching the rough face of the cliff, Krista moved cautiously downward, grateful for the stretches of hand-railing protecting the seaward side of the footwalk. She glanced downhill, toward the beach, and stopped in her tracks.

Unexpected beams of light danced along the sandy surface below. Krista had not considered the police. Of course they would be guarding the beach entrance against unwanted publicity seekers. Now she was glad she had not brought a light. Although the police would be more intent on intruders from the outside, it was certain they would question anyone, regardless of which direction they came from, found on the beach.

She wanted to meet no one. . .except Broderick.

Taking a deep breath in an attempt to slow her racing heart, Krista gathered the corners of her collar close to her cheeks and shivered. The damp cold was as chilling as ever. She moved on.

Soon Krista's feet touched the soft sand. She inched her way carefully along the base of the cliff. On the seaward side, the waves broke directly over the rock. Here, a wide stretch of sand separated the cliff from the bay.

Krista inched further and found the crack she was searching for—the mark in the mounded rock formations that told Krista she was close to her cave. As a child she had found several caves, but this one was her special place. As far as she knew, it had never been found by anyone else. She had never shared its existence with anyone but Broderick.

Placing her foot in the crack, she reached to feel a series of cracks, like miniature steps, that ascended an odd number of feet above her head.

She had come here often enough, but never at night without a light to see her way.

Grasping the gritty holds, she pulled herself up, a step at a time, and flattened herself against the protruding stone. She stopped and listened, the sound of her breathing loud and raspy in her ears. The policemen were moving away. She could hear the low whisper of the wind and the faint rumble of the ocean.

Krista took a breath, set her jaw and felt for another handhold.

At the top, the rock was smooth, leveling to a space large enough for a half-dozen people to stand. Pulling herself over the edge, Krista stopped briefly, then slid forward and located the ledge and yawning void of the drop-off into the cave.

Levering herself through the space, she rolled onto her stomach and dangled her legs over the side. For one horrifying, split second, her body was free in the inkiness of space.

Krista struck the cave floor with a sand-muffled thump and fell backward, heart pounding, onto the smooth sand. She lay sprawled on the floor, hearing the sounds of her breathing and heart intensified in the vacant confines of the cave.

Above, a faint patch of stars could be seen through the mouth of the cave. A barely discernible moan whistled past the exit as a whisper of wind was caught among the rocks.

Krista shivered. Sliding backward, she located the rock wall and leaned against it, placing herself into position to watch the irregular patch of sky.

If it was Broderick she had seen at the house, he would come here. He would know where to find her. If not—Krista tugged her collar closer to her cheeks—she would locate the handholds she had avoided when entering the cave and make her way back to her rooms.

If it had been Broderick. . .what would she say? Or do? Broderick had always had a strong influence on her. She shuddered suddenly and began to wonder at the impulsiveness of what she had done.

Krista pulled her legs up and wrapped her arms around her knees.

Broderick Penton. . .tall. . .dark. . .older than she. He had been her gymnastics and diving instructor. . .and so much more.

She tilted her chin high in the air, trying to get a grasp on all her feelings. Broderick had turned her world upside down, made it gloriously happy—and agonizingly painful. Her chin sank back to the warmth behind the zipper. She frowned as memories filtered through her mind.

Krista focused on the few sparks of light that shone through the cave opening. They blurred and she rubbed her palms into the tears that had somehow started. She would not cry. She could not cry.

A scuffling noise brought the points of light sharply back into focus, then a figure blackened the entrance.

Krista's heart gave an erratic series of thumps, and she stood quickly as the person followed her earlier maneuver and landed close by on the sand.

A flashlight snapped on and the beam of light flashed across her feet, tracing its way to Krista's face.

Blinking, Krista shielded her eyes from the glare.

His voice, husky, rolling the way she remembered it, came from the vague outline beyond the blinding light. "How long have you been here, Kristy?"

"Not long. Since I. . .thought I saw you."

The beam fell to her feet and Broderick moved closer, tall—almost overwhelmingly so—a strong presence in the small cave.

Her thoughts were confused. She should not have come. A

shiver overcame her.

The flashlight found a resting place above her head on a jutting outcrop of rock. Then his hands, large and strong, descended to grasp her shoulders.

"Did you think I wouldn't come?" he asked. "After I heard about your uncle's death?" The deep tones were whisper soft.

"I," she began hesitantly, licking salt from the edges of her lips. "I didn't know."

His hair, still dark, had silvered more at the temples. Broderick hated that obvious banner of his years. Krista had considered it a distinguishing feature—one that added rather than detracted. His blue eyes, dark in the uncertain light, appeared to be drinking her in. He was watching her so earnestly, gazing at her eyes, her nose, the width of her cheek. . .her lips.

Her mind reeled with questions. . .and accusations.

She should not have come. He was going to kiss her, she knew, and she. . .should not, but . . .she. . .

Krista turned her head and Broderick's lips connected with her cheek. She thought Broderick stiffened, but the impression was so fleeting, so smoothly passed, that Krista disbelieved her notion the instant it shot through her mind.

"I've not forgotten," Broderick whispered, his arms tightening as if the past two years had been a dream.

Krista studied the man whose earnest face was inches from her own. "Why, Broderick?" she asked. "Why did you leave me?"

"I explained. . ."

"In that letter? I tried to believe it was a forgery—a fake. But you were gone," she said. "You left no trace for me to follow."

"I was afraid you would try. As much as I ached to have you

find me, I sincerely believed leaving you was best."

Krista's voice rose in intensity. "How could you when you knew how I felt?"

"Our ages. . ."

"You knew I didn't care!" she uttered, pushing away from his grip. "To me you were heaven and earth. . .all I needed to breathe. . .and you were gone."

Broderick sighed and shoved his hands into his pockets. The action flexed his shoulders, emphasizing the muscles beneath the lightweight jacket he wore.

Broderick's look scanned the rocky walls about them as he admitted regretfully, "I am fifteen years older than you."

Palms flattened against his chest, Krista said, "What is age when there was love such as we had between us?"

His gaze returned to hers. "I do love you, Kristy; I always have. When I left. . .it was for your best interests." He reached for her, his tone soft and caressing. "You can see I'm admitting how wrong I was. . .so very wrong. I've been waiting for you to come back—watching for you. But you never came home."

"You've been waiting for me?" Disbelief colored her tone.

"Yes, Kristy, I have."

Krista edged away from his touch. "Tell me how you got past Nan, into the house. I can't believe she would have allowed your entrance."

Permitting the distance Krista put between the two of them, he smiled slightly and said, "As much as she tries, the woman can't be everywhere. With all the additional servants hired to accommodate your guests, it was fairly easy to enter unnoticed."

"The security. . ."

He chuckled. "One man recognized me and let me in without bothering to consult the guest lists." Pausing a moment, he said, "You must know this. . . . Once I realized the terrible mistake I made in leaving, I tried to find you."

Krista's eyes narrowed fractionally as she scrutinized him. "Did you?"

"Yes. But by then *you* were gone." Broderick shifted in the enclosed space. "I tried for months. I looked everywhere I could think of, questioned everyone we knew. I even went to all the places we'd dreamed of going together. I looked everywhere."

Krista's voice became level. "I'll bet you did."

Quiet came between them. There was a searching pause.

Broderick tilted his head ever so slightly and asked, his voice deep and slow, "What exactly does that mean?"

"It means, Broderick," Krista's chin lifted, "that if what you desired most for me, as you so aptly explained in that letter you sent, was the chance for me to reconsider, to not be pressured by your presence, you would not, under any circumstance of persuasion, have taken the money."

Silence descended heavily around them. Broderick's expression froze.

His voice was flat. "What are you getting at, Kristy?"

Broderick was the only one who had ever called her that. It had always made her feel so very special. But now. . .

Krista's lips were thin, her fingers twisting into tight balls at her side. "Uncle Anthony bought you off, Broderick—paid you to get out of my life."

Broderick's mouth opened, but no sound denounced her accusation.

"What really hurt," Krista paused, and the pain was evident both on her face and in her voice, "was that you took it."

Broderick's face darkened as he grasped the realization of what she was saying.

"Who told you such a thing?"

"Was losing me worth. . .a quarter of a million dollars?"

"But I. . ."

"Don't deny it. I saw the canceled check. . .and your signature on the agreement." Krista hugged her arms to herself, her eyes shifting upward, then coming back to search out Broderick. She struggled against the emotions within her. "How long was it before you realized you could have had much more if you married me?"

"That's pretty low."

Her eyebrows rose, tempting him to deny it. "How long?" she repeated.

He grimaced, his fingers curling inward. "I needed the finances and the recommendation. Anthony gave me no alternative. I would have been blacklisted for any decent job. It was that or bow out quietly, pleading the difference in our ages."

"Instead of coming to me?"

"I admitted I made a mistake."

Stepping toward her, Broderick reached for Krista. "Let me prove it to you, Kristy. Once this funeral is over we'll go away together—just the two of us, alone. You always wanted that before. There's no one left to stop us now. Don't let this come between us."

"There've been two years and a lot of pain come between us. Two years." Her head shook. "It's all over. I'm a different person. There's nothing left."

"You can't mean that." Broderick's grip tightened on her arms. Krista flinched at the pain. "We can," he stressed, "pick up where we left off."

Krista attempted to ease away from his touch. "Too much has happened in that time, Broderick. You can't deny that this ever happened. . .that you never left."

"You can't find it in your heart to forgive me?"

"Let go," she said, pulling at the increased discomfort of his grasp. Fear gripped her. Being here, alone with Broderick, was a mistake, a grave mistake.

"I won't let you go, Kristy." Broderick's grip tightened as he urged her closer. "You were mine once and I want you back. Anthony Mariano played havoc with our lives and I won't let anyone do that again." She felt the warmth of his breath tickle her cheek, her hair. His fingers dug into the soft flesh of her arms. "We'll be together. I won't let anyone else have you."

Krista's thoughts whirled, her breath coming in quick, sharp gasps. This was not the Broderick she knew. He was changed, alarmingly so.

Krista gave a whimper of pain and twisted, attempting to loosen his grip. "You're hurting me," she cried.

Unexpectedly Broderick's hands came away. Krista stumbled back.

"Forgive me," he spoke hastily. His hand reached toward her. Krista shied from his touch. "I didn't mean to hurt you. I've just missed you so terribly much."

Krista circled Broderick, making for the cave exit.

"I frightened you," Broderick realized. "That's the last thing I wanted to do to you. I apologize. Just say you haven't written me off entirely. Give me a glimmer of hope." His gaze was earnest in the insufficient light. "I do love you, Kristy."

She had to get away. "I. . .I need time to think."

"Of course. I came on too strong. It's just that," his hands came out imploringly with a sound of dismay, "I've missed you so very much. These two years have driven me crazy, wondering what happened to you." Broderick reached into his jacket pocket. Krista's gaze sharpened. He withdrew a small card that he handed to Krista. Hesitantly, Krista reached for it. "This is where I'm staying," he told her. "My room number is on the back.

"Call me, " he urged. His eyes darkened as they bore into hers. "I won't leave town without you beside me."

Krista swallowed. "It's not wise for you to come back to the house," she managed to say. "Nan or one of the older servants might see you."

"I'll stay away if that's what you prefer for now."

"I have to go." She edged closer to the handholds. The card found its way into her pocket. "Now. Nan will be looking for me."

"Certainly." Broderick nodded in agreement. "I wouldn't want to cause difficulty between you and Nan."

His fingers touched the flashlight. The beam of light sliced the darkness, pinpointing the crack in the rock wall that was Krista's steppingstone out of the cave.

"Here, I'll give you a leg up."

"I can make it," Krista said.

"I insist," Broderick replied, tucking the light into his pocket. The beam flashed chaotic rays of light into the darkness as he moved.

Boosted effortlessly through the opening, Krista scrambled into the fresh, salty night air. She breathed deeply.

Flashlight extinguished, Broderick came after her with a silent stretch and tensing of his athletic form, easily pulling himself out of the darkened cave.

Krista gave a shake and straightened her jacket. She saw no security people or lights and heard no sound except the faint whisper of Broderick's jacket and the ever present, muted background of waves.

Broderick's voice was close to her ear. She barely restrained the flinch that twitched her muscles away from him. "I'll go down first."

With the merest hint of sound, Broderick landed on the sand below. Krista could see the outline of his arms as he reached toward her. "Jump," he said softly. "I'll catch you."

Squatting low, Krista thrust herself over the edge. . .and

landed in Broderick's arms. He did not release her.

"I'll be in my room all night," he said, tightening his hold. "Call me. We'll talk." His words were accompanied by a firm, unavoidable kiss that left Krista with no doubt of what he expected her to do.

Breathlessly she said, "Leave before someone sees you. I've got to get back to the house." It was the coward's way out, she knew. She should tell him exactly what she thought of his actions. . .and of the very important Someone who had changed her life. . .but she was afraid of the consequences. She had seen Broderick's displeasure toward other people. Her arms still ached with the imprint of his fingers.

"If you don't call, Kristy, I promise I will find out who is responsible."

Krista nodded, desperate to leave. Then she turned and left Broderick where he stood.

Her hands were cold. She was cold. She had been such a fool. Her body shivered as she relived the demand of Broderick's kiss. Her fingers scrubbed roughly across her lips. She should never have gone to the cave. Never.

Krista hurriedly retraced her steps up the path to the mansion. What had seemed to be hours had been one at the most, and every room in the estate appeared to be lit. Krista received the impression that more people had arrived in the short eternity she had been with Broderick.

A clustered handful, ignoring the night chill, were making use of the large patio and steppingstones that extended off the ballroom. Keeping well into the shadows, Krista skirted the boundaries of light, using the meticulously trimmed hedges as a screen.

A sharp spurt of fear shot through her when the back door did not come open at the first twist of her wrist. All she needed at this point was to have to enter by the front door! Giving the handle a rough jerk, Krista stumbled back as it suddenly opened, then fled through the opening just as a low shout escaped a man's throat. One of the housemen rushed toward her.

Apologies wreathed the short man's expressive face when he realized who was standing in the feeble glow of the hallway light. "I'm sorry, Miss Johnston. I didn't realize who you were and, well, Miss, we have had some crashers, and I thought since someone was using this door. . . ."

"That's fine," she assured him, grateful that Nan would not have to become involved, yet piqued over the thought of how many people must know her now—if not by name, at least by sight. There was a short pause before she asked, "Are there many security personnel working the grounds?"

"Yes, quite a number. Of course we're dressed to blend with the guests," he indicated his evening clothes.

"Have you all been shown a picture of me?"

"Yes. Miss Carr asked that you not be disturbed if we see you." An expression of regret flooded his face.

"So if you were shown a picture of anyone else, you could keep that person from entering the grounds?"

"We would certainly do our best."

"Come with me," she instructed as she turned to hurry along the hallway to the staircase.

The man came along silently and waited outside her suite at her request.

Moving directly to the high chest of drawers in her bedroom, Krista knelt and gave a tug on the bottom drawer. It slid out smoothly to reveal an assortment of clothing articles which she pushed to one side to expose a large, face down photograph.

Krista's jaw set. She turned the photo face up.

The picture had been taken two weeks before Uncle Anthony made his move. She had been so happy. It showed in the trusting smile she was giving her. . .fiance.

Broderick.

I will always love you was inscribed across the bottom.

Krista found a pair of scissors and the inscription came off first. Then she cut herself out of the picture, leaving a squared portion that contained only Broderick's smiling face.

Satisfied with the results, she returned to the man who stood at her door.

"This man," she thrust the clipped photograph at the security guard, "is not to be allowed on the estate. One of you let him in tonight without consulting the guest list." Her hand raised to forestall any apologies, and she shook her head briefly. "It's not a problem now," she said, "but I don't want the man to return. His name is Broderick Penton and the last he was seen was on the beach. I'm assuming he has a car on the grounds somewhere, so you're to permit him to remove it. However, once he is gone, he is not to be allowed to return. Is that understood?"

"Yes, Miss Johnston. Will there be anything else?"

"No. That is all."

The short man straightened as high as his stature permitted and gave a little bow of acknowledgment to her instructions. Expressing his profuse apologies over any inconvenience Mr. Penton may have caused, he assured Krista that the man would not enter the estate grounds again.

Krista brushed aside his words and with a weary sigh, closed the heavy door and leaned against it. Her lower lip trembled from pent-up emotions that quivered to escape. With her coat still zipped to her chin, Krista sank onto the tapestry covered sofa. Her numbed fingers fumbled with the dial on the telephone. She sniffed as a tear trickled down the side of her cheek. Krista swiped at it and regarded the glistening drop that coated her fingertips.

The telephone rang in her ear and a man answered the call.

Krista smiled a softly tremulous smile.

"Jake," she said and paused. "I miss you."

—14—

The muted sounds of Krista's telephone roused her from a chaotic sleep full of disjointed dreams of Jake and Broderick mingled with nameless faces, dark caves and roads that led nowhere.

Hazily, Krista attempted to push aside the threads of dreams that remained. The telephone rang again. She reached for the lampswitch and frowned against the sudden light, focusing on the hands of the small clock placed on her nightstand: 2:13. Krista stretched for the telephone and muttered a groggy, "Hello. . ."

"You will never get away with it"

"What? . . ." Krista's voice recovered a semblance of normalcy from its sleep-drugged state. She shifted upward in her bed, pushing her hair from her eyes.

"You know what you have done," the voice whispered.

Fear stabbed through Krista at the cryptic words as her mind shifted into gear. The voice was raspy, high-pitched, altered. Icy cold clutched at her insides.

"Who is this?" Krista's heart thudded. The voice did not answer. "What do you want?"

"I almost had you once. I will not miss the next time."

The words hovered on the line and echoed in Krista's ear. There was a slight sound in the background, then a series of clicks. The dial tone returned.

Her heart beating erratically, Krista managed to replace the receiver in its cradle. She stared wide-eyed about her, clutching her covers protectively under her chin.

Who could it have been? Not many people knew her private number. Krista trembled as she remembered the sound of the voice, odd and menacing. What would she not get away with? What had she done? What did he mean?

Her fists stuffed sheeting into her mouth. That car *had* intended to force her off the road!

Krista smoothed base makeup across the bridge of her nose, carefully covering traces of the faint freckles that always came out when she was in the summer sun. She glanced nervously toward the high double window in her bedroom. There was no summer sun today. Dull grey overcast filled the sky—typical coastal weather for this time of year.

Krista stilled her fingers and considered what was expected of her this day. The funeral. She exhaled. It meant she was expected to come out of her self-imposed seclusion and be seen by people who knew or were acquainted with Anthony Mariano.

Krista twisted the cap onto the bottle. If a show was what they wanted, she would give them exactly that: Cool elegance and reserve.

As Krista smudged on eyeshadow, she saw how bloodshot her eyes were. After the phone call she had been unable to sleep. But she had discovered the Psalms in her frightened vigil. Pausing, she still marveled over the peace that had filled her as she read hungrily, "The Lord is my light and my salvation; whom shall I fear? The Lord is the defense of my life; whom shall I dread?"

A sudden and unexpected feeling came over her. Krista stopped, her hands dropping to her lap.

How did she really feel about Uncle Anthony's death? Was there actual sorrow or remorse on her part or merely. . . what?

Rubbing her palms together, she thought about it. She had feared him, his power that dominated her life. . .and how she had had so little say about her choices. Yet. . .through all his dominance of her affairs, had not Uncle Anthony seemed to try to protect her?

Krista stared at herself in the large mirror of the dresser. Where would she have been if Uncle Anthony had not bought off Broderick? She would never have been happy. Broderick used people. Her eyes pressed shut momentarily, then opened. Broderick had used her. Uncle Anthony had been right.

Krista's throat tightened. What had she been looking for when she went out to meet Broderick? Answers to her questions? She had received them, bitter as they were.

She had thought that once Anthony Mariano was out of her life and she had put all his business affairs behind her, the Mariano family burden overshadowing her would be gone.

But now something. . .sinister had crept into her life. The shadows weren't ending.

"Father, please help Krista know what you want her to do with her life." The words of Jake's prayer echoed in her mind.

What *was* she going to do?

Did God really care so much about the details of her life?

Krista gave herself a tiny shake and began to smooth shadow across the other eyelid.

She had been making plans for the estate. An idea had come to mind sometime during her sleepless hours, and she had called her lawyer earlier to begin inquiries. The man had stuttered a bit over her unexpected call, but Krista had ignored it. She knew he had been the weak link in keeping her Colorado residence a secret, but she sympathized with the man. Anthony Mariano had been relentless when he chose to be. Her uncle had probably made the lawyer's life miserable.

Jake would approve of her plans.

Krista's features softened at the thought of him. Deep

inside she wished he were here. She would have felt safer if he was with her, but Krista's mouth quirked and tightened with resolve. It was better he was not, if for no other reason than the gossip headlines: Reclusive Heiress and Mystery Man— Who Are They?

Krista dragged the brush through her hair and twisted the ends upward. She couldn't risk that notoriety. Diamond crusted combs held the roll in place. She was beginning to look expensively elegant. . .just the effect that would help protect the Krista Johnston she wanted to be.

A light tap sounded on the outer door.

The housekeeper was dressed in a dark, tailored skirt and jacket. White lace edged the high collar of her blouse and— Krista was taken aback by the sudden realization—Nan was an attractive woman. Strange how she had never taken note of that before.

Nan's silvered, dark hair was looser than usual, fuller around her face, lending a soft, pleasing quality to the efficient housekeeper.

"Steven is in the library," Nan announced. "You are expected to meet him there, then go on to the ballroom for the memorial service. There is a semi-private cubicle for the family. Afterward, we will all travel to the cemetery. Mr. Mariano," Nan's voice developed an unexpected tremor that was quickly brought under control, "requested that I sit with. . .the family."

Krista slowly straightened, shifting her shoulders so that she could look directly at Nan.

"If there is," Nan continued, "a problem with that. . .I will understand."

"No," Krista's head gave a slight sideward shake. There was a tiny frown etched between her brows. "If that's what Uncle Anthony wanted, then you are to do that." Her inflection drew out the next syllables. "Was there a particular reason?"

"Perhaps. . .he thought you might want me there."

88

Krista's brows rose. She refrained from comment.

Pursing her lips over her thoughts concerning Nan, Krista slid her feet into black, spiked heels. Tiny rhinestones swirled a pattern across the toes of the shoes and swept along the sides to the heels. She took a few practice steps.

Directing her comments, but not her attention, to Nan, Krista said, "Since I can finish dressing myself, you may as well go to the library. I won't be long," she added, noting the expression on Nan's face. That particular expression usually precluded the "don't be late" lecture.

Krista glanced into the dresser mirror, settled the small hat on her head, and tugged its lacy, short veil into place.

Nan left.

Short lengths of diamonds dangled from Krista's ears. A matching necklace encircled her throat, and a large diamond ring completed the set. Her black dress was severe enough to be in fashion. The lightweight, silk-lined jacket slid smoothly into place.

Mariano Estate Heiress.

Krista's lips thinned from their natural fullness as her jaw tightened.

She reached for the black leather clutch with its diamond latch, turned, and headed for the door.

—15—

The halls were subdued. There was a hush over the mansion. Krista glanced at her watch. She had a few minutes to spare before she and the rest of the "family" were required in the ballroom.

Her footsteps whispered down the thick carpet, stopping before a deceptively simple redwood door.

She wavered, heart beginning to pound in deep, rhythmic succession. A quick inspection of the hallway revealed no one in sight. Krista attempted to swallow, and her fingers began to shake as she reached to clutch the large, curved brass handle and give it a silent twist downward.

The door swung open and Krista teetered on the threshold, gripping the handle as if the inanimate object could ease the chaos in her thoughts and feelings. With weak knees, Krista stumbled through the opened doorway and managed to close the door behind her.

She drew a shuddering breath, then took the few, faltering steps needed to turn and view the paneled room.

There were cases with Uncle Anthony's favorite books, each volume bound in tooled leather. A rich brown leather sofa stood against one wall. Brass lamps sat on marble topped tables. The carpet was deep and forest green, and the accents scattered around the room echoed the color.

Her heart gave a restless thump. Krista's eyes squeezed shut, then reopened. Anthony Mariano's desk was huge—an antique from previous generations. What family secrets it must hold. . . .

The last time she had seen her uncle, he had sat at that desk; his stern, once handsome face stiff with resolute decision.

Nan had been. . .there—Krista pinpointed the spot with her gaze—standing a respectable distance from her employer. Nan had always been beside Uncle Anthony whenever there was a dispute, agreeing with him and upholding whatever decisions he made. She was the perfect employee, never questioning Anthony Mariano's decisions. . .no matter how great or small. His word was law, and Nan accepted it as such.

As had Krista, for the most part. . .until the day Anthony Mariano had shown her proof that Broderick, her love, had accepted a quarter of a million dollars instead of her heart.

Painful memories twisted her mouth. Her glance lept from the accusingly vacant area of the desk to the framed painting on the wall. The picture was different now, one of a haunting, misty, coastal morning. The other had been a striking mountain scene.

The force with which she had heaved the crystal paperweight had knocked the original painting from the wall, creating a dent in the paneling.

Nan had been horrified at the blatant destruction. Krista remembered her grim satisfaction at having provoked something other than passivity from Nan. Only Uncle Anthony's restraining lift of his hand had prevented the woman from leaving her dutiful position.

Never had Krista shown a display of temper before.

Never had she reacted violently to her uncle's dictates.

Never had she spoken to Uncle Anthony again.

Krista drew a slow, deep breath into her lungs. "What," she thought evenly, "would I tell him now if I could?"

She was not certain anymore.

On the far side of the study was a door, recessed and dark.

Anthony Mariano's private entrance to the library. As a child Krista had used the passage. Few others did. The door had been her way of arriving at the library with a minimum of fuss. The library was accessible through this doorway via a balcony, or by entering through the hall off the main foyer downstairs.

Of course, Krista had never used this entrance when Uncle Anthony had been at home. However, he was often gone on business trips. That was how she met Broderick.

Throughout her school years, she had had a number of private tutors. As her gymnastics and diving instructor, Broderick Penton had been given lodging on the estate. For seven years he had provided Krista daily instruction in the gymnastic arts. Her love for him had grown from an acceptance of his presence as another of her teachers, to infatuation, to dreams of a life together. He remained even after she began attending classes at a nearby college.

But Broderick had been here, waiting for her return home on the weekends so they could resume her studies and. . . Krista thrust those thoughts away.

The balcony overlooking the library was made private by strategically arranged potted plants. A chair, small table and lamp made for secluded reading. . .and clear hearing of whomever might be speaking below.

Steven was speaking, as Krista entered the balcony. There was a questioning murmur from Linda. Krista parted the fronds of a fern, a slight frown on her face, and leaned outward to view the large, bookcase lined room beneath her.

Steven paced agitated steps in front of the marble fireplace. Linda was standing helplessly nearby, her hands pressed against the back of a padded, wing-back chair. Nan was nowhere to be seen.

"You don't understand!" Steven whirled about and leaned emphatically toward Linda. His voice lowered, but was no less intense. "These people don't play games. I'm in trouble—

deep trouble. If I don't get my hands on a sizable amount of money soon, they won't hesitate to make me wish I had."

An exclamation of exasperated disgust thrust itself from Steven's throat, and he spun around to shove his hands against the fireplace mantle.

Steven stared at the flames flicking upward in lazy, hungry waves of color. His hands dropped and he faced Linda, his movements slow and deliberate. His eyes were dark, his face stonelike, haggard.

"They threatened me—and they were not idle threats. I would *kill*," Steven said, "to get the money I need."

Linda's gasp was loud in the book lined room. "You don't mean that!"

Steven's lips drew to a fine line.

The plant shushed softly as, wide-eyed, Krista removed her hand and stepped back. Her fingers slipped about her throat where the pulse had begun to beat in hasty rhythm.

Had Steven been the one who tried to run her off the road? Desperation could change anyone, but...Steven—capable of ...*murder?*

Krista leaned outward once more in time to see Nan enter. Her cousin remained where he had been standing, his expression hard. Linda, whitened, was in disbelieving shock.

The housekeeper's glance swept the room. "Is Krista not here?" she asked.

Linda's mouth dropped, and she took an unconscious step back, clutching shaking hands over her mouth. Her eyes darted from Nan to Steven.

At the first sight of Nan, Krista hurried along the protected narrow balcony and then slowed her steps to a uniform pace as she descended the carpeted, open staircase.

"I told you I'd be on time," Krista spoke, a clipped sharpness coming to her words. "You needn't have been concerned." She paused at the bottom, steeling herself to look from one person to the other.

Steven's mouth tightened further, his brows edging together. His hands shoved themselves into the pockets of his tailored suit, and he turned his back on Krista.

Linda's barely masked, horrified glance flicked upward to the balcony, over to Steven, and on to Nan before coming back, for the briefest of seconds, to rest on Krista.

"I suggest," Krista said, "that we be going. The sooner this is over the better it will be for all of us."

The memorial service was long and tedious. Admiral Epstein was eloquent in his speech concerning the business triumphs and contributions Anthony Mariano made in advancing goodwill to his fellowman.

The room was full of people. Krista, Steven, Linda, and Nan sat to one side of the great room, protected from curious viewers by the veiled cubicle and massive flower arrangements sent to honor the late Anthony Mariano.

Krista shifted in her chair, recrossing her legs and repositioning her black clutch across her knee. She felt rather than saw Nan's covert observation.

Admiral Epstein droned on. Anthony Mariano's achievements had not been few, and it seemed Admiral Epstein intended to relate each in detail.

Steven, seated next to her, was abnormally quiet. Krista stole a glance at him from the corner of her eye. He stared straight ahead, a stony expression deepening the corners of his lips into a downward twist. Krista had never seen her cousin like this.

It scared her. Steven was the carefree one, the one who laughed at life, the one who played. She had grown accustomed to that, and as much as it irked her at times, she preferred that to this. . .and the thought that he might be desperate enough to run her off the road. . .or make threatening phone calls.

Linda's fingers crept over to entangle themselves with Steven's. Krista looked away.

The minister who had worked with Uncle Anthony's many local charitable causes was exchanging positions with Admiral Epstein. With the change of people, Krista cast her gaze around the room—what she could see of it—and observed the people who had come to pay their last respects to her uncle.

A few people openly stared at the shrouded, improvised room, knowing the heiress sat inside. Krista could almost verbalize their speculations. Her lips thinned, and she drew a silent breath that was followed by a tight-mouthed sigh.

Krista frowned, tipping her head slightly as her gaze moved upward to the balcony of her rooms, the corners of it shadowed as always. A sliver of light shown through the uppermost portion of the drapes—a place where shortly before there had only been darkness. Her fingers tightened around her purse, and her brows formed a deeper furrow.

Who? . . .

Then she smiled the tiniest hint of a smile at herself. She was jumpy. Of course it was the maid straightening her room.

The minister was praying, obviously done. Startled, Krista wished she had paid attention to his short sermon—she felt the need of spiritual comfort more now than ever.

After the prayer, the pastor gave the announcement that the graveside services would follow for the immediate family and for those who were requested to accompany the family. Nan's chin dropped. Silent tears glistened on the housekeeper's face. Yet the woman was composed as only Nan could be. The housekeeper touched the tip of her lace-edged handkerchief to the trails of moisture on her cheeks. But Steven sat stiff-faced and silent, his eyes boring holes into nothing in particular.

—16—

Outside it was damp and chill, and the graveside service was brief. An early fog settled in, requiring careful driving on the chauffeur's part on the way back to the estate. Steven made a number of quips about the events scheduled for that evening. For Krista it was a relief to see him relax after the unexpected outburst earlier. Yet, she viewed him with caution, unable to entirely dismiss his threats and actions.

As soon as they returned, Krista went to her rooms. Giving a groan of relief, she sank onto the sofa in the sitting area. She kicked off her shoes and curled her toes under, then up.

At least that was over.

Conflicting emotions assailed her. She no longer knew how she felt now that Anthony Mariano was no longer a part of anyone's life. Somehow, and unexpectedly, given the way she had felt the past two years, she experienced a queer sense of loss for the man who had dominated her life.

Giving a sigh, Krista focused her thoughts on other matters.

Her fingers pulled the combs from her hair. The veiled hat already lay next to the phone on the end table. Krista carefully laid the combs inside the hat. She would have them replaced in the safe later. . .along with the other jewelry. The unclipped earrings were dropped beside the combs, as were the necklace and ring.

Ruffling her hair, Krista combed through it with her fingers, loosening the confining twist. The tiny wisps of bangs fell onto her forehead, and she brushed the strands back before reaching for the telephone.

She wanted to talk to Jake. Her conversation with him the night before had left her homesick for Colorado and McIntyres'. The long distance ring sounded several times before it was answered by a male voice.

"Jake?" A puzzled inflection colored her tone.

"Hi, Krista. . . .No, this is Darrell. How are things in California?"

"Spooky. Sobering. There was more to that car trying to run me off the road than I wanted to believe. Also, Steven is in some kind of trouble that has him nervous and making rash statements. There's more, but I won't go into it. I am a bit skittish. Where's Jake? Is he on the floor?"

"Uh. . .no. . ."

Darrell's suspicious sounding answer strung out and Krista frowned at the intonation. "Where is he, Darrell?"

"By now. . .probably closer to you than me."

Krista faltered, her words forming slowly. She clutched the receiver tighter in her hand and asked, "What does that mean?"

"It means he's flying to California to be with you."

"I told him I didn't want him here." Helpless irritation slipped into her words, and Krista shifted her position on the sofa.

"I know what you told him. I even reminded him of that fact, but Jake has a tendency to be bullheaded, and when the man gets an idea into his head, there's no stopping him. Besides, he said he knew you'd been crying when he talked to you, and he was sure his presence would calm any of your protests."

Krista pressed her palm to her forehead, then, permitting it to drop to her lap, she lifted her head to stare unseeingly at the fireplace. Lips pursing, she almost smiled.

"When will he arrive?" Krista asked.

"I knew you wouldn't be upset with us for too long."

Krista permitted that smile. "You guys are," she closed her eyes and shook her head, "terrible. You don't listen to a word I say."

"We listen, but we make our own decisions. You know Jake is pretty patient about most things, but he felt he needed to be with you."

"So, what time will his plane arrive?"

"I'm afraid you'll have to check flight schedules there. Since Jake didn't give me any details, I really don't know." Darrell added, "He could use a ride to your place."

Krista could visualize Darrell's twisted grin at the all-too-obvious hint. Her smile deepened. "I'll be there."

"That's the way." he encouraged. "Oh, and Krista. . ."

"What?"

"Hurry back. We all miss you here. I've been working on that piece of music just for you."

Smile sobering, Krista spoke softly. "We will. Both of us. Real soon."

Replacing the receiver, Krista sat a moment longer.

Jake. Coming here.

Krista's fingertips pressed against her mouth, and she admitted she was glad. . .*really* glad.

Standing upright, Krista began planning—meeting Jake's flight, preparations for a room, notifying Nan.

Krista smiled at the vision of Jake's frame draped across the too short loveseat in his office. He wasn't picky. . . .

"So, . . ." A male voice said, "I wondered why you hadn't given me a call. I'm truly disappointed in you, Kristy."

98

—17—

Startled, Krista spun sharply, eyes wide.

"Broderick!" she exclaimed. "What are you doing here?"

The man completed his entrance, dropping the draperies into place. "I wanted to see you," he replied, unperturbed. Dark eyebrows raised as one hand slid to his pocket. "I assumed you would be delighted to see me. Obviously," Broderick moved with a casual step toward her, rounding the table, "you are not thrilled. You disappoint me, Kristy. I thought we were going to be together again, just like it used to be," his brows creased slightly and his emphasis became a subtle caress, ". . .only better."

Krista was backing steadily away from Broderick's advancing form and placed a chair between herself and him. Her heart thudded in fear. How? How could he have gotten past the security guards who were watching for him?

"Is there really another man after all?" Broderick asked, stopping just opposite Krista and the chair. "I couldn't help but hear your conversation." His head shook with a sad wistfulness. His voice became a velvety, disbelieving question. "How could there be anyone else? Ours was a singular and captivating love. You can't give it up so easily, so casually. Don't you remember what we had?

Krista began to quiver. Her mouth worked. An unbidden sob suddenly tore from her throat, and her hands came down as fists on the back of the chair. "Yes," she choked. "I *remember*. I remember being frantic over losing you—racing to your rooms only to find there was nothing left. No clothes.

No pictures. Nothing to remind me of you—not even the scent of your cologne. Even that was gone. *Gone.*"

Krista's words slowed as she studied the dark features of the man on the other side of the chair—the silvered hair, the deep blue eyes, the lean jaw.

"Do you know what that did to me?" she asked. "Can you possibly imagine how that affected me? And then to find that our *love* was so special that—you left me for two hundred and fifty thousand dollars."

Krista's chin rose defensively, her words clear in the silent room. "Impressive figure, wasn't it? You got what you wanted, only now you find it wasn't enough, and you want more." Her features sharpened in self-defense. "I'm sorry. I haven't more to give you, Broderick. You've taken all you're going to get from me."

Broderick's head tilted with contemplation, Krista's barrage of words seeming not to have affected him.

"Who is this friend you have coming to town?"

Krista stiffened. "I don't see how that's any of your business."

Broderick pursed his lips in a swift gesture of disregard. "I've always preferred to be informed about my competition," he replied.

Krista blinked in disbelief, then shook her head. What was he saying? What did it take to get through to him? "What are you talking about?"

His brows shifted. "Then you were just playing with me last night?"

"I. . ." Her mouth came open and she hesitated, torn by her need to be honest with him. "I thought I wanted to see you," she admitted. "I felt I needed to. . .to satisfy any last doubts I might have had." Krista interjected her next words before Broderick could reply. "But I was wrong. All those questions had already been answered by your signature on a cancelled check. Seeing you only confirmed what I already knew."

"I admitted I made a mistake," Broderick said. "You made me believe we could start over."

"No, Broderick. You made yourself believe we could start over. You heard only what you wanted to hear."

"I see," he said.

Broderick took a step to the side of the chair. His proximity and the reasonable tone with which he spoke sent a spurt of anxiety through Krista. She knew Broderick, knew the passion of his emotions. She did not trust him. Broderick was an achiever and did not tolerate being thwarted.

"How did you get in my rooms?" she asked, and backed to keep distance between her and Broderick.

"There isn't any place I can't go on these grounds, if I want to badly enough." A hint of smile touched his lips. "We discovered all the hiding places together. . .didn't we?"

"If you don't leave right now," she paused briefly, her gaze narrowing, "I will call security and have you removed."

Broderick smiled.

"No you won't," he said, "because you don't like scenes, and you wouldn't want all that attention drawn to yourself."

Krista shifted her shoulders back and stared at this man. She had come back to face this very thing. She would not run away now. . .nor let this man dominate her with half-whispered insinuations of yesterday.

Krista swiftly circled Broderick, moving just out of reach, and stretched her hand for the telephone.

Her fright filled gasp was harsh. The hand that covered hers pressed the receiver firmly back to its cradle. Broderick's fingers were hard and tightened with the threat of pain.

"You don't really want to do that." Broderick's breath warmed the side of her whitened features.

Krista turned to stare at him, her wide, grey eyes pinned by the darkness of Broderick's. She trembled.

"Kristy. . ." Broderick spoke softly, his hand moved to her

cheek. He frowned. "You're not afraid of me?" His tone was edged with disbelief.

Broderick's fingertips traced the curve of her chin. "There's no need to be afraid of me," he assured her softly. "I'm the one you love; I know that. I'll make you remember it. We've had good times together. We will again." His dark eyes stared into hers. "I'll make you forget the past two years. It will be as if they never occurred. We'll love each other, you and I."

"I will never love you, Broderick." Krista's voice quavered, but her look sharpened. "You betrayed me when I needed you most. You're no better than. . .than Uncle Anthony—making your plans and using me for your own means. All I meant to you was a bank account."

Broderick frowned, his face a study of disconcerting emotions.

"You can't give up what we had together."

"You did that over two years ago," Krista replied.

Growing in confidence, she touched the telephone with the tips of her fingers. "So, will you leave quietly or do I call security?"

"I won't let you love someone else."

Krista said, "There's nothing you can do about that. I've already fallen in love with Someone. Someone who means more to me than you ever did—or could."

The lean jaw she had once loved tensed. Broderick's lips thinned, then, unexpectedly, softened. He opened his mouth, his words accentuated by the sudden look in his eyes.

"We'll see about that."

Broderick backed away from her, then turned toward the door.

"My mind won't be changed." Her voice shifted a half note higher. "The two of us have nothing left between us."

Broderick shocked her with a smile—an unconcerned bending of his lips that plainly spoke his disagreement. Krista's jaws snapped together. "Broderick. . ."

A knock at the door stopped Krista. Her mouth dropped open.

The smile never left Broderick's face as he curled his fingers around the doorknob and opened the door.

"Do come in," Broderick encouraged the speechless housekeeper. Nan's jaw dropped with a tiny, sharp intake of breath. "I'm just leaving."

Broderick disappeared and Krista stared in stunned apprehension at the empty space he had left behind.

The housekeeper's gaze watched Broderick's progress down the hall.

Krista squeezed her eyes shut briefly, giving a heartfelt, mental groan. She threw up her hands as Nan's focus returned to her.

"Don't say it," Krista begged. "I don't want to hear it. He was here, he is gone, and I pray that's the last of it. Let him leave the way he came." Her hands dropped, and she shook her head wearily. "What did you need?"

Nan hesitated, arranged her composure, and began to speak. "The reading of the will. . ." she started.

". . .will have to be postponed." Krista's interruption gave no opportunity for Nan to reply. "I have other plans."

Shrugging out of her black jacket, Krista tossed it on the end of her bed.

"People, naturally, are concerned," Nan replied, trailing her mistress. "The reading of the will is essential to keep business running smoothly and permit the various corporations to adjust to any new changes." The housekeeper retrieved the discarded clothing. She shook the folds from the material. "It has been scheduled for this afternoon, Krista. You cannot just ignore this."

Krista paused in her rummaging through her chest of drawers. Her head gave a tiny shake along with a small, defensive frown. "I'm not. It's just that something important has come up. And please leave my clothes alone," she said, pinning Nan with her gaze before drawing a pair of jeans from the drawer. "I will take care of my clothing myself." The drawer shoved closed.

"Are you..." Nan wavered, regarding the jacket in her hands before laying it carefully on the end of the bed, "going to be with Mr. Penton?"

Changing clothes quickly, she gave Nan the benefit of her open gaze.

"I have a guest arriving soon. Please see that he has a room, preferably in this wing. No, it is not Mr. Penton," she inserted as Nan's eyes appeared to narrow. "It's Mr. McIntyre from Colorado. He will be arriving on what I'm assuming is the next flight, if memory of flight schedules serves me right; they haven't been altered in my absence, and," she pulled a face, "the fog doesn't set in too heavy. I would like the room ready within the hour. Don't fuss. He's not particular."

Krista shoved her blouse tail into the waistband of her jeans. She asked, "When will the rest of our guests be leaving?"

Nan's hands folded. "Some have gone already. Others will leave soon, I'm sure. Jennifer Farlow, however," the stiff shoulders twitched, "has insisted that she will not leave without seeing you."

Krista heaved a sigh, rolling her eyes skyward. Jennifer had visited Mariano Estate sporadically with her parents, who were old friends of Uncle Anthony. It was supposed, since the two girls were close in age, that they would become good friends. Such was not the case. Krista could barely tolerate the superficial mannerisms of the girl.

Krista grimaced. "Please spare me the effort. I have more important things to do than listen to her rattle on about all her latest conquests."

"She's being very insistent."

"So am I."

Krista returned to the previous topic. "As far as the reading

104

of the will is concerned, I apologize for the inconvenience of having to reschedule it, but I imagine everyone will be able to find the time later—after I return from picking up Mr. McIntyre."

"Surely one of the servants could pick up your friend."

"Yes, someone else could." Krista passed a brush through her hair. The upswept style she had worn earlier gave the strands body and it fluffed out, curving around her jawline. "But," she continued, "I don't *want* someone else to pick him up." The brush came down on the dresser top. "*I* will do that." A practiced hand erased the majority of the makeup, toning the colors and dramatic sculpting to a more natural glow.

Glancing at her watch, Krista stated, "I have to go. I'm certain you'll make all the necessary explanations." Her lips tightened for a brief moment. "You're good at that. Besides, I won't delay the reading the of will by more than an hour or two, so no one ought to be terribly put out."

Dragging her denim jacket off its hanger, Krista returned to the living area where she retrieved her black leather purse and removed the wallet. She stuffed the wallet into the pocket of her jacket.

Nan came as far as the doorway between the two rooms. The housekeeper watched in silence, her face composed, resolved.

A frown notched between Krista's brows. She was being a dictator and she was sorry for the need, but she knew she must take a strong stand. Otherwise, Nan would try to dominate her, and, above all else, Krista could not allow that to happen.

Krista wondered briefly at Nan's reaction once the woman was informed of her plans. Not that it. . .or anyone's reaction mattered. Nan would accept it as she had accepted everything that happened through the numerous years she'd remained a faithful employee for Anthony Mariano and a disciplinarian for Steven and Krista.

Steven would have to accept her plans, too.

Turning abruptly on her heel, Krista left.

The temperature was warmer than it had been earlier, but the high overcast remained, shrouding the countryside with its grey pall. The smell of salt was in the air, and Krista could hear the ever present, muted thunder of waves beating the rocks on the seaward side of the peninsula. Two seagulls cartwheeled overhead, screeching as they soared.

Krista glanced furtively about her, half expecting to see Broderick emerge from the shadows. But no one approached her. She hurried on toward the garage.

Opening the side door, Krista flipped the lightswitch, flooding the interior of the building with fluorescent lighting. She located the key box, punched in the combination, and opened the door to extract the key for the truck—an older model, bought for use in the rough, redwood terrain to the east, and perfect for her needs now.

Stopping momentarily at the gate, Krista let the security man know, tactfully but firmly, her displeasure at Broderick's appearance in her quarters.

The man, apologetic and perplexed over Broderick's ability to move around the grounds unseen, promised to spread the word of what had occurred and take added measures to prevent Mr. Penton from entering the estate again.

Krista put the truck into gear and began the descent off the bluff, wondering at what would follow. Broderick was up to something. He was disciplined enough to make good any subtle threat. . .especially if he had incentive.

Krista's mouth twisted to one side. Broderick had incentive . . .even if it was connected to false hope.

I will not miss the next time. The words echoed in her mind. She thrust at them—pushing the raspy voice from her thoughts. *Lord, help me to be strong, to honor you in all of this. I am afraid.*

Krista found the airport busier than normal. She suspected

the current events at Mariano Estate had a lot to do with that. Entering the parking lot, Krista carefully positioned the big truck into a slot.

Her eyes were drawn upward by an insistent, droning roar. If that was the plane she thought it was, she had barely made it to the airport in time. Jake was here.

Her spontaneous smile could not have been contained had she wanted it to be. Hurrying, Krista drew on her jacket as she neared the doors to the airport.

People milled about the rooms, spilling through the outer doors on the airfield side. There, a waiting area was fenced off for people meeting new arrivals.

Krista started in that direction. . .then stopped short.

Reporters! Complete with cameras and microphones and local television insignia, they were interviewing, of all people, Jennifer Farlow.

Diverting her steps, Krista quickly placed a wide support column between her and Jennifer and the *paparazzi*.

Why here? *Why now?*

Pressing her back against the curved surface of the column, Krista stared at the crowds. She stretched her chin and swiveled her head to observe Jennifer once more. The girl was laughing and waving the reporters away.

"What's the matter, Kristy?" a male voice drawled. "See someone you know?"

Krista recoiled violently, slapping her hand to her mouth as it dropped in horror.

Broderick's smile was lazy and amused as he pressed his hand above her head, against the column.

The realization of her precarious position drained the color from Krista's face. A hollow dread filled her. "Why are you here?"

Broderick's dark brow rose thoughtfully.

"It does make for an awkward situation, doesn't it? To find there's not one, but two people here who could recognize you and call you to the attention of those gossip hungry reporters."

Broderick's head had tilted in the direction of the newspeople who were approaching other famous or wealthy looking people.

"I am truly amazed," he continued, "that so few people recognize you. It seems a shame the public is being denied the opportunity to meet the heiress to the Mariano Estate."

"Are you threatening me?"

Broderick looked as if he were about to laugh. "Me? Threaten you? I love you, Kristy. I would only protect you. Of course, I would insist that you were my fiance and that the heiress to the vast Mariano fortune would be foolish to look at a humble instructor of gymnastics." Broderick tipped his face close to hers.

Krista's lips tightened; her insides churned with growing frustration.

"What are you planning to do?" she asked.

"To protect you from your own folly."

"Uncle Anthony has already done that for me."

Her chin lifted with a sideways tip. No matter what Broderick did, she would not run and hide. She would be cautious, but not afraid. *The Lord is my...salvation; whom shall I fear?* The thought gave her strength. "I'm beginning to see," she said, "the blessing of Uncle Anthony's actions more and more."

Straightening from the column, Krista waited until Broderick removed the symbolically possessive hand. Her steady, grey gaze pinpointed him.

"I hope," she said, "to never have to say this again." Krista paused, then continued, her voice strong. "There is nothing left between you and me, Broderick. What we once had cannot be redeemed, and you are deluding yourself if you think it can. I do not love you, nor will I ever love you again.

It's over. If *you* care anything for *me*, don't try to intimidate me, just leave me alone."

Lips tightening in disgust toward Broderick, Krista turned sharply as a voice over the intercom announced the arrival of Jake's flight. Keeping her face averted from anyone remotely resembling a newspaper or television reporter, she wove her way through the crowd toward the doorway Jake would be entering.

Broderick dogged her footsteps, and her anger changed to frustrated speculation. What was he planning? But even as she asked the questions, she knew time would bring an answer.

A spontaneous, worried frown tightened her features.

How would Jake react if Broderick caused a scene, carried out his threat to publicly label her his fiance?

"Krista!" a feminine voice uttered in exultation. "What are you doing here?"

Krista halted as pursuasive fingers plucked at her jacket sleeve, tugging her around.

Jennifer Farlow—blonde, pretty, petulantly indulgent, and happily surprised.

Krista plastered a smile on her face as she automatically answered Jennifer's urgent question. "I'm meeting a friend." Krista scanned the incoming crowd, but did not see Jake among the few people trickling through the doors. She added, "What about yourself?"

"I'm seeing Mother and Father off—urgent business to care for, you know. They can't be away from home long. I stayed," Jennifer's hand squeezed Krista's arm, "because I wanted to see you." She continued without taking a breath, her hand fluttering dramatically upward. "But that house-keeper of yours won't let anyone near you." Jennifer tilted her head with a smooth and immediate seductiveness as the line of her focus altered to just beyond Krista's shoulder. "I see you've managed to get around Nan, however. Introduce me to your friend, Krista."

Krista's smile deepened with a touch of incredulous hope as she artfully dodged Broderick's intended, possessive grasp.

"Surely you remember Broderick Penton," Krista replied, her hand moving in Broderick's direction.

Jennifer's face, which would have been comical if Krista were not searching for a way out of her present situation, became one of blank disbelief. Jennifer stared from Krista to Broderick and back to Krista, managing, with effort, to retrieve her jaw from its slack position.

Snaring Krista's forearm with the tightened curve of her fingers, Jennifer jerked Krista a half dozen steps to the side.

"What are you doing?" Jennifer hissed, her sharp eyes flickering between Krista and Broderick's relaxed form.

Broderick crossed his arms. He tipped his head. His lips bent patiently upward.

"Are you crazy?" Jennifer persisted. "No wonder Nan's been so adamant about who sees you."

"Jennifer, believe me. I have no desire to be near that man. I have found myself in a very difficult situation, though, and I would like to appeal to your sense of romance and adventure."

"My *what*?" She stared at Krista, then, frank, perplexed curiosity slowly changed to the glitter of secretive impishness. Jennifer's eyes narrowed as a smile began to touch the corners of her mouth. "You're meeting a man," she decided. Her shapely shoulders twisted away from Broderick. "Or is it a girlfriend and you'd rather not have the competition?"

Tact was not one of Jennifer's strong points. . . .

"It's a good friend of mine. . .male. . .and. . . ." This was no time for hesitancy. Jennifer was hanging on every word, "I have not asked Broderick here. He's being very insistent and will not take 'no' for an answer. He thinks since Uncle Anthony is gone we can pick up where we left off. We can't, but I can't convince him, and I can't get rid of him either."

"And you want me to distract Mr. Penton while you meet this male friend of yours."

Krista never thought she would see the day she would be grateful for Jennifer's flightiness toward the masculine gender.

"Would you?" Krista asked. "I don't know what to do, short of making a scene. With all these reporters here, I'm afraid of what Broderick might do."

Jennifer's smile was fraught with sympathy, and she patted Krista's arm. "Still like to stay in the background, huh? Well, let me think." Jennifer let loose a tiny, contemplative breath and tapped the center of her lips with the tip of her index finger as she took note of the people around them. She straightened, then leaned conspiratorily toward Krista. "Whatever we do, we'd better decide quickly. I think your friend has arrived."

Krista followed Jennifer's line of vision and saw Jake weaving through the crowd, searching for her. Catching her eye, he smiled and lifted a hand in greeting.

From the corner of her eye, Krista also saw the lift of Broderick's hand as it raised, caught the attention of a reporter, and pointed at Jake. A small group of people mobilized instantly—a woman with a microphone, a cameraman, and a handful of others wielding pads and pens and bloodthirsty expressions.

—18—

Krista gasped in mesmerized horror as the throng of reporters swooped upon Jake as vultures to their prey. A microphone was shoved at his face, the woman reporter behind it determinedly firing questions at the startled man.

Others chorused similar questions, voicing their opinions of this man's relationship to the Mariano Estate heiress and asking, demanding, verification of their accusations.

"Is it true that you are a close, personal friend of the woman who has recently inherited the Mariano business holdings?"

"Why did you delay until after the funeral to be with her?"

"Tell us about this mystery woman. . . .Who is she? What is she like?"

"How did you meet her?"

"Tell us about yourself, Mr. . . ."

"Are you romantically involved with Miss Mariano?"

"We've heard rumors of an engagement. Are you the lucky man?"

People gaped. Jake's blank look flashed through the surging throng, then through a parting of the crowd to where Krista stood, paralyzed by Broderick's traitorous act.

Broderick, pressing close to Krista, placed his arm around her shoulders. She jerked away from his touch.

Jennifer, still close by, spoke hastily to Krista, touching the girl with a quick snatch of her fingers when Krista would have rushed toward Jake.

"Stay here," Jennifer ordered. "I'll see what I can do."

Elbowing a path through the crowd, Jennifer's voice and laughter somehow transcended the decibel level of the room. The reporters' questions eased as Krista's childhood playmate prated contradictory facts to what Broderick had insinuated to the persistent gleaners of news and gossip.

Snaring Jake's arm through the crook of her own, Jennifer beamed at Jake and his bemused expression gave way to a haphazard smile.

Jake's eyes lifted once more to Krista's forlorn agony, then concentrated on the confusing disturbance before him as he took note of Jennifer's actions.

"You've got the wrong fellow, ladies and gentlemen," Jennifer was saying. She paused to flirt with the cameras. "Of course he's not Miss Mariano's fiance. He's my—" her smile was an expressive gleam as she leaned into Jake, "*very* good friend."

A hasty protest sprang to Krista's lips, but she immediately swallowed her words. Casting a furtive look about her, Krista retreated against a column and waited helplessly.

Jake had begun to realize what Jennifer was attempting to do and placed his hand over the girl's grip, flashing her a conspiratorial smile.

"So if you will excuse us, we really must leave now. Miss Mariano is expecting us, you know. Poor darling. . .she's having such a difficult time with this entire ordeal, and she wants so much for us to be with her."

An instantaneous surge of questions regarding Miss Mariano spat around Jennifer, but she waved them off with a shake of her head and smiled more glowingly.

"You know how Miss Mariano treasures her privacy. No, I'm sorry. You dear people will just have to forgive me. I couldn't tell you anything that you don't already know. I mean, what are friendships for, anyway? We must keep our little confidences to ourselves. That's only fair."

"What's the name of your fiance, Miss Farlow?"

Jennifer let loose a peal of laughter. "Who said I was getting married? . . .*Yet*."

Jake yielded to a smile, and Jennifer began to tug him through the parting crowd.

Krista sprang forward to bisect the couple's path at the doorway only to be wrenched back by Broderick's rough jerk.

"I won't let you get away with this," he growled.

Krista studied the play of frustrated anger moving across his face.

"What are you going to do?" she asked, her voice surprisingly calm and distinct. "Turn the reporters on me now?" Pulling away from his grip, her chin tilted with a final look, then she turned and raced toward the doors.

Thrusting herself through to the outside, Krista scanned hurriedly about her and spied Jennifer's entreating wave from beyond the first row of cars in the parking lot. She hurried across the paved drive and squeezed between two closely parked vehicles.

Jennifer, breathless with triumphant delight, said, "I didn't know where you'd parked."

Barely acknowledging her, Krista hurled herself into Jake's arms. They clung to one another. His arms were strong and they tightened before his hands slid to her shoulders, holding her away from him just enough to look into her eyes.

The somber depths of green compelled a heartfelt response from Krista. "I'm so glad you came," she said.

"You must hurry," Jennifer urged, returning Krista to the urgency of the moment. Her hands swung expressively wide. "You've got a brief moment, but your Mr. Penton may pull some other stunt." She shrugged—a minute, quick movement. "Or the reporters could get suspicious. They are that way, you know."

"How can I thank you, Jennifer?" Krista asked.

"Save your thanks. Take your man. It was the least I could do." Jennifer's tapered fingers wiggled as her finely shaped brows lifted. "At times frivolousness can be a timely advantage. Now get out of here," she shoved at the two of them. "I'll take care of your Mr. Penton and," her voice lowered in earnest supplication, "I'll see you at the estate?"

Krista's brow creased with a curiously contrite expression. She had never dreamed Jennifer would do anything like this for her, that Jennifer cared enough to do this for her. "You will," she assured her and hesitated as Jennifer waved her away and beelined back toward the airport terminal.

"Come on," Jake tugged Krista by the hand. "Where's your car?"

Krista saw Jennifer cross the drive and catch Broderick by the arm just as he emerged from the building. This was no time for a confrontation between Broderick and Jake. Broderick was angry. He had never tolerated losing.

"This way," Krista commanded and pointed, snatching at Jake's arm and dragging him into a quick jog.

"That was some arrival committee," Jake remarked with a quick, over-his-shoulder observation as they hurried between the rows of parked cars. Jennifer had succeeded in slowing Broderick to a certain extent. They could hear her continuous, entreating chatter drifting behind them.

"I didn't know what to think when I saw all those reporters," Krista admitted breathlessly. "I didn't know what to do."

"Who was tall, dark, and handsome with the possessive grip?"

"Oh, Jake!" Krista stopped, gasping for a breath, pain flitting across her features. She gulped a breath of air and swallowed. "What can I say? I have to explain."

"Later."

Jake's index finger jabbed at a location behind her, and Krista whirled to see Broderick closing in in spite of Jennifer's attempts to impede his progress.

Krista burst into a run, skirted the car next to the truck and fumbled in her pocket for the keys. Jake snatched them from her grasp, paused as he unlocked the truck door, then practically lifted Krista bodily onto the bench seat.

By the time she was able to right herself, Jake had started the engine and was jamming the stick shift into reverse.

Glancing out the back window of the pickup, Krista saw Jennifer sidestep hastily, attempting to drag Broderick with her. The man glowered at their escape. His piercing glare speared Krista as she craned her neck only to lose sight of him behind a van as Jake turned the truck toward the exit.

Krista turned toward Jake. "I am. . .so sorry for all of this," she began.

"No," he contradicted, and paused just long enough to wrap his free arm around her and pull her close beside him on the seat. "I'm the one who's sorry," he said. "I'm sorry you ever had to come back to this place. But most of all, I'm sorry you came alone." His grip tightened fleetingly.

Jake braked to a stop at the pay booth. Determined reassurance gleamed in his eyes. "But that's changed. You're not alone anymore. . .and I'm not leaving until you come back to Colorado with me."

Jake's arm came away while he dispensed with the necessity of parking lot fees.

Jake's hand returned to the steering wheel, and he placed the truck in gear, entering the highway in accordance with Krista's directions.

"Fill me in," Jake said. "Who was the girl?"

"Jennifer? Jennifer Farlow. An. . .old friend." The words came out in puzzled wonder.

"You didn't have that charade planned?" Jake asked. "We're fortunate she's a quick thinker. And," he added, catching Krista's eye, "that tells me how well you've guarded your background." Jake frowned. "Doesn't anyone outside your small

116

circle of local friends and associates realize who you are?"

"I hope not." She frowned over the thought. Krista glanced out the window at the passing view of redwoods and coastline, absentmindedly sliding her fingers down the edge of her jacket as she contemplated Jake's question.

"What else has been going on?" Jake questioned.

Sudden fear flooded her as she recalled the threats.

"Steven is upset about his financial problems and is making rash statements. Also, I received a threatening phone call. Someone *is* trying to kill me." Krista shuddered and gripped Jake's arm. "The caller practically admitted he was the one that tried to run me off the road. . .and told me he wouldn't miss next time."

"He?" Jake asked. "It was a man?"

Krista shook her head. "I don't know. The voice was strange—like it was disguised—hoarse and whispery, high-pitched." She shivered at the remembrance. "I was so frightened."

Jake was frowning and silent, absorbing what Krista had told him. He asked, "Why haven't you contacted the police?"

"What would I tell them? An unknown car tried to run me off the road? . . . .Someone called me in the middle of the night? Besides, the estate is crawling with security and, quite frankly, I don't want or need the extra publicity."

"I'm doubly glad I came now," Jake stated.

"Me, too."

Under Krista's direction, Jake drove the truck through the small coastal town. Krista watched him take in details. When they approached the sweeping, strategic curve along the townward edge of the bay, Krista pointed past the windshield toward her childhood home.

"Mariano Estate—where I grew up." Krista looked at him. "That's where I played, studied, was shaped with the anticipation of one day becoming her mistress. . .and all it means to be just that."

Jake's features lowered in contemplation. Unexpectedly, he steered the truck to the side of the road and paused to study the view of the bay. His eyes took in the sweep of water and the austere elegance of Mariano Estate. The steady hum of the motor vibrated the cab of the truck.

Krista watched Jake, a spark of worry flitting through her. Her fingers slowly crept together and laced themselves in her lap.

"Isolated, isn't it." It was a statement from Jake, rather than a question.

"Yes."

"You didn't have much opportunity to make friends, did you?"

Slightly taken aback, Krista allowed her puzzlement to show.

"I'm talking about real friends, Krista—the kind you plan and dream with—the kind you share your innermost secrets with—the girlfriends. . .the boyfriends."

Her bewilderment changed to pain. She thought of Broderick. . .and Jennifer. Then, she hesitated. . .but had to know. . . .

"Darrell said you were coming because you knew I had been crying last night."

"I came," Jake said evenly, "because I care about you very much." He strove to catch her wavering gaze. His fingertips touched her chin and gently lifted it until her eyes met his. "Darrell, Carrie—all of us at McIntyres' care for you because of the person you are, not who you are supposed to be." He stopped. His gaze intensified with a gentle, unspoken plea. "Let me into your life, Krista. Don't hide things from me. I'll help. . .and I'll try never to hurt you."

Krista bent her head to study her hands as she slowly circled her thumb across the knuckle of the other.

She lifted her glance toward Jake. "I do trust you."

Squeezing her hand, Jake said, "From what you've said, there are some things going on here that neither of us understands. I wish I had come with you in the beginning." Then he added, "The man at the airport. . .he was, at one time, someone very special."

The comment caught her off guard. Her eyes lifted toward Jake. "Yes," she admitted.

"I think I understand why any man who once knew you would not easily, nor willingly, give you up." His hand rested lightly on top of her stilled fingers. "Don't worry about it, Krista. We'll discuss that later. I know you want to." His hand dropped away. "But not now. For now, I just want you to know. . .that no matter what happened between you and him it makes no difference in how I feel about you. We're going to work this out together."

Krista's look flickered over Jake. She frowned, attempting to absorb the reality of his words. Her gaze crossed the bay to the imposing building on the point of land, then back to the man who sat so close and cared, so unconditionally, about her.

Jake gave a slow smile as a glimmer of sober amusement began to glow in his eyes. He raised his arm and gave a thrusting flick of his wrist.

"Shall we go slay dragons at white castle beyond, fair lady?"

Jake's abrupt sense of the absurd brought a suggestion of a smile to the corners of Krista's lips.

"Are you my knight in shining armor?"

Mock surprise traced upward to Jake's raised brows. "Is there any other?"

"No." Krista's voice was quiet. "No, there is no other."

Jake's voice quieted, too. "It's time to go." He pushed in the clutch and shifted into first.

—19—

At the gate, the guard waved them past. There were, perhaps, fewer vehicles remaining than when Krista left. She could not be sure.

Jake pulled into the car filled garage and clicked off the ignition. His hands came to rest at the top of the steering wheel, keys dangling between a thumb and forefinger. He gave a cursory glance to the length and depth of the building around them.

The keys jingled. Then Jake looked at Krista. "Know where I might find a good cup of coffee?"

Krista stared at him. Her blank look slowly evolving into an uncertain, disbelieving smile. "You want coffee," she said, repeating Jake's words. She could not quite believe that Jake was not interested enough to comment on Uncle Anthony's private automobile collection. Broderick had been fascinated. . . .

"I assume there is a kitchen here."

Jake was not Broderick.

Retrieving the keys from him, she smiled.

"It's not Pete's coffee, but the kitchen staff does make a good brew."

Jake smiled and opened the truck door. "Let's go."

Krista accepted the grasp Jake offered, replaced the keys in the security box, and let his hand fold over hers.

The immense gymnasium was vacant and Krista's voice echoed against the ceiling in response to Jake's lifted brows.

"There is also a workout room, a soundproof rifle range, and three racquetball courts. Guests put those particular rooms to use more than the gymnasium."

"I expected a pool," Jake commented.

"Both are very nice," she said. "One has a high dive."

"Did you swim much as you were growing up?"

"I could have been in diving competition. I was told I had Olympic possibilities."

"And you didn't try?"

"I'd worked too hard at keeping in the shadows. There was no way I'd subject myself to the scrutiny of an Olympic hopeful."

"Do you like basketball?"

She laughed at the sudden gleam in Jake's eye. "I've played. I'm pretty good one-on-one."

"Want to later?"

Her smile deepened, and she tightened her laced fingers between his. It was so good to have him here.

"Sure. Why not? Then, if the pool is unoccupied, we can do some swimming." Depressing the release bar, Krista thrust open the door to the house.

"Swimming. . .swimsuit." A look of dismay washed over Jake's face as he suddenly halted. The door swished shut behind them. "I left my luggage at the airport. In all the fuss, I never gave it a thought."

"No problem," Krista said. "I'll send someone over for it. This way," she moved forward and led the way under the stairs.

"Your private entrance?"

"Of a sort," she admitted. "I can get to my rooms, the family's kitchen, the gym, or outside via this hall. I've used it a lot."

"Especially when there are people around?"

She looked at him. "It's convenient."

Turning up the stairway, they entered the hall that

121

connected the Mariano living quarters. There was no one in it. Krista was glad. Confrontations and explanations were the last things she wanted right now.

Soon her life would be easier—as soon as the reading of the will was over. Another hour or so would begin the process that would have Mariano Estate and all the Mariano holdings out of her hands forever.

"Make yourself at home," Krista said, as they entered her apartment. Slipping out of her jacket, she draped it over the arm of a chair. She reached for the telephone. "I'll have coffee sent up and have Dean get your luggage. Do you have receipts so he can identify it?"

"Here," Jake produced his ticket stubs and laid them on the end table next to her hat and the telephone. His brows lifted as he nudged the sparkling pile of diamonds.

"Part of my rich heiress act," Krista said. "I should have had them put away, but I was in a hurry to meet you."

Dialing a series of numbers, Krista watched Jake turn from the end table and wander casually about the room, pausing at an odd item or two. Nothing, she noted, kept his attention long.

Jake turned back to face her just as she gave instructions for the retrieval of his luggage and an order for coffee, ". . .in something sturdy, please." She paused. "That would be fine. Thank you."

Krista smiled apologetically as she hung up. "I would make coffee myself, but, as you can see. . ." she shrugged helplessly.

"I appreciate the offer." Jake grinned as he stepped toward her. "You can make coffee for me when we get home." His voice softened. "I'll bring the eggs."

Krista just looked at him, her smile sobering as she shook her head. "I'm sorry about that, Jake. It. . .wasn't a very good morning for us, was it?"

"That wasn't your fault," he said, laying serious hands on

her shoulders. His gaze studied her own, as if to read her innermost feelings.

"The man at the airport. . ." Jake's brows rose with the unasked implication.

The dismay over Broderick's inexcusable tactics and the rush of feelings that suddenly overwhelmed her were stronger than she anticipated. In spite of herself, Krista stiffened. Her withdrawal caused Jake to tighten his grip in a silent attempt to draw her back.

Krista's chin dipped and she stepped back from Jake's grasp, turning to walk several steps away.

"Let me in," Krista heard Jake's voice say gently, and she turned to see regret darken the corners of his eyes. And the regret was more painful than the hurt Broderick had caused.

"Broderick," she said. "His name is Broderick Penton."

"He was special to you."

"He was. . .my fiance."

Jake's hands slid to his pockets. "Go on," he encouraged.

There was no condemnation in his stance, no hardening of his eyes. They were soft, reassuring, patient.

"Uncle Anthony disagreed with the match and bought Broderick off."

"And now?" Jake's eyebrows rose.

She sighed. "Now he thinks since Uncle Anthony is gone that we can pick up where we left off. That fiasco at the airport was of his making. He did it to scare you off—to give you a taste of what it might be like to. . .interfere."

"I don't scare easily."

"What happened at the airport is minor compared to what he could do. He could ruin you. You would suffer. McIntyres' would suffer. . .because of me. That was why. . .I told you you didn't want to become involved with me."

Jake's hands came out, palms upright. "What does he hope to gain from all of this?"

Krista gave a short, humorless laugh with a pathetically twisted smile. "Me."

"He thinks you would want him? After what he did?"

"I believe, in his warped manner of thinking, he is working on the assumption that if no one else can take the heat, I will be satisfied with whomever is left. Which, of course, would be him." Her hands lifted about her, encompassing her rooms, the entire household. "He wants the estate, the cars, the business holdings." She dropped her hands. "He wants an heiress." An independent gleam flickered in Krista's eye as an index finger tipped upward. "However, he's working on a false assumption. Soon I will no longer be an heiress."

A speculative look crossed Jake's features and a half smile touched his eyes. "What have you done? Or should I ask?"

"I think. . ." Her fingers pushed through her hair as a light, inescapable scowl sprang to her face. "I hope. . .you will approve." Turning, she ran her hand across the smooth tapestry of the back of a chair, then twisted again to face Jake.

Krista's heart had begun to thud deep and hard and her mouth dried as her thoughts raced over the plans she had created. It would affect so many people.

Jake covered the space between himself and Krista and grasped her hands with his own. "Whatever you've decided, if you want to be certain about whether it's right, let's pray about it. Jesus Christ cared enough to die for all the wrong things you've done; you can be certain He cares enough to help with the right things."

Krista studied the lean strength that held her hands—the thumbs that circled, then soothingly squeezed.

"I'd like that," she said, "because I'm certain there will be others who will violently oppose what I've planned." Her head tilted back so she could see his face.

"Does it matter?"

"It might."

A light tap sounded and Jake's focus flickered over her shoulder toward the door. His head tilted in that direction.

Krista raised her voice, "Who is it?"

"Nan," came the clear answer.

Krista smiled. "Come in," she said and turned just enough to watch the door swing slowly open.

Nan entered with a ladened serving tray.

"On the table would be fine, thank you." Krista slipped past Jake, brushing against her jacket. She snared the collar and draped it over her arm, then reached for Jake's claim tickets and the hat containing the diamond jewelry.

"Don't bother to pour," Krista addressed Nan, then asked, "Which room is being prepared for Mr. McIntyre?"

"The blue room," Nan answered, carefully lowering the tray onto the table. "I trust that is within your specifications," Nan's lips tipped ever so slightly upward as she acknowledged Krista's guest, "and will be sufficient for Mr. McIntyre's needs."

"Excellent choice, Nan. Thank you."

Nan permitted herself to nod once, then asked, "Will there be anything else?"

"Yes," Krista said. "Here are Mr. McIntyre's claims for his luggage and," she handed over the slips of cardboard, then the jewelry, "please put these back in the safe. I won't be needing them anymore."

"With your permission, the reading of the will is to be within the hour."

Subconsciously lifting her chin, Krista smoothed her coat over her arm and caressed the course material with the flat of her hand.

"Better now than later. In Uncle Anthony's office?"

"Wherever you prefer."

"The office will be sufficient."

"If there is nothing else?"

"Nothing," Krista said, stuffing her hand into the wide jacket pocket to remove her billfold. She drew in a sharp breath. Shoving her fingers deeper into the slot, she cried, "My billfold's gone!"

"What do you mean?" Jake asked. "Did you have it in your pocket?"

"I put it there when I left to meet you." Krista's face lost all color as her jaw dropped with sudden realization. "I must have lost it at the airport. . .when Broderick was chasing us."

"Broderick?" Nan questioned.

"Yes," Krista's teeth snapped together. "Broderick. The man's been following me. If it hadn't been for Jennifer's quick thinking, reporters at the airport would have had a field day with Jake. Yes, Jennifer was there," she answered Nan even as the woman's mouth came open.

"Jake. . ." Krista's troubled eyes sought his. "If Broderick has my billfold, he'll know where I live—how to find me. He could cause no end of trouble. He won't leave me alone; I'll never be able to escape him."

Jake had moved toward her even as she spoke, and he squeezed his fingers into her tense shoulders.

"You don't know for certain that Broderick found your billfold, and who else out there realizes Krista Johnston is the Mariano heiress?" His frown softened to a gentle lecture. "Don't jump to conclusions, Krista. Your billfold could still be in the truck."

Krista stared at Jake. She wanted to believe what he said, but she couldn't.

"And we'll call the airport," Jake continued, interrupting her thoughts, "to see if anyone has turned it in there. We'll exhaust all logical possibilities before assuming he has it. Then," he shrugged, "we'll go from there." Jake's thumb caressed the sharp edge of Krista's jaw. "Even if it isn't in either place, you can't be certain Broderick has it." A reassuring smile lifted the corners of Jake's lips. "It will turn up."

"I will call the airport," Nan said, already thumbing through the phonebook she pulled out of the end table drawer. After much explanation and what seemed an eternity, Nan was informed that the billfold had not been turned in at the airport.

"I'll check the truck," Jake said, sliding his hand down Krista's arm and giving her fingers a consolatory squeeze.

"I'll go with you."

"The reading of the will. . ." Nan began.

Krista opened her mouth to postpone it once more, but stopped. Better to get it over with, once and for all.

"Just let me know when everyone is ready," Krista replied, and Nan silently scuttled from the room.

"She's very dedicated," Jake commented as he reached to help Krista into her jacket.

"She likes things her way," Krista said without much thought, then added, "But, I suppose you could attribute her attitude to dedication." With a quick movement, Krista brushed strands of hair away from her face and turned to Jake. "Except for two weeks out of the year, Nan does not leave the grounds unless she has business in town. . .which is seldom. She does almost everything over the telephone."

"Vacation?" Jake asked.

Krista preceded Jake to the door. "Nan goes to Detroit every year to see an elderly aunt of hers."

A light tap on the door caused Krista and Jake to glance at each other. Krista opened the door.

"Mr. McIntyre," Steven beamed. Little of the day's earlier melancholy appeared to remain. "So nice to see you again." A hand shot out and dangled mid-stretch for Jake's grip. He was alone and Krista wondered briefly where Linda was.

Krista felt rather than saw Jake stiffen beside her as he grasped Steven's outstretched hand. Something about Steven

127

really bothered Jake.

"I had no idea you were planning to visit our humble lodgings here," Steven continued. "Are you being treated well? We simply must show you as good a time as you bestowed on Linda and myself when we visited you."

"I'm fine," Jake assured him, adding slowly, "I appreciate the thought, though."

Steven waved fingers of dismissal and turned his attention to Krista. "When is the reading?" he asked.

"Didn't Nan see you on the way out?"

"No." His head shook with a slight edging of earnestness around his eyes. "We must have bypassed each other somewhere on the stairs or in the hall or something. I need to know, Krista. It's very important."

Krista hesitated. She had not forgotten the desperate look. . .or his words in the library prior to the funeral.

"Soon," Krista said, and added, when the look in his eyes intensified, "within the hour, in Uncle Anthony's study. Honestly, Steven, whatever it means to you can't possibly be critical between now and the next sixty minutes. I'm certain Uncle Anthony didn't leave you in the lurch."

Steven speared her with an uncharacteristically sharp glare for an instant, realized Jake was watching, and altered to a fractured smile. "I will see you then," he replied, backing out of the room, moving with modest haste down the hall.

"Your cousin bothers me," Jake said, staring at Steven's retreating form. "I'm not sure if it's due to his attitude when he ran us off the road or what, but he disturbs me."

"You're right. There is a problem," Krista inserted. "But it's with him. . .and it may be more extreme than I realized." She stopped as Jake secured the door behind them.

"What are you talking about?"

"I overheard a discussion between him and Linda earlier this morning," Krista said as they moved to the stairwell. "He's in debt, and I'm positive it's linked to his gambling. He prefers the game tables," she added in reply to Jake's expression. Their footsteps whispered as she moved ahead, and they descended the narrow back stairs. "It's serious, and what he said scared me. It was so unlike Steven."

Jake reached out and stopped her progress, his eyes dark with suspicion. "What exactly did he say?"

"He said," her eyes met Jake's, "he would kill to get himself out of the situation he was in."

Jake looked grim, and his brow knotted.

"What about this phone call you say you received? Could that have been Steven?"

"I don't know," Krista answered. "Like I said before, the voice wasn't recognizable. It was strange, frightening. The problem is, not just anyone has my telephone number. It's unlisted, and I rarely gave it out. There are only a small number of people who have access to it."

"Which means," Jake said, "that whoever is threatening you—is someone you know."

Krista's face was a mixture of bleak fear. "I. . .know. But that's not all," Krista added, almost unwillingly as the reality of her danger became clearer. Jake's expression sharpened as he waited for her explanation. "I think it's a possibility that I may have been followed here by the car that tried to run me off the road."

—20—

They searched the truck thoroughly, but the billfold was nowhere to be found. Krista crossed her arms and gave Jake a worried stare as he slammed the truck door shut.

"This still doesn't mean Broderick has it," Jake said, wrapping his arm carefully around Krista's shoulder and pulling her closer to him. She allowed herself to be drawn into his arms and rested the side of her cheek against his shoulder. It was comfortable there.

"What am I going to do if he does, Jake?" She tilted her chin upward so she could look into his greenish-grey eyes. "He'll make life miserable. I know Broderick. He can be horribly vindictive." She shook her head and said softly, "And I thought I was in love with him once."

A sense of uneasiness chilled her. Edging away slightly, she said, "It scares me—involving you."

Jake's grip tightened, and he tugged Krista closer. "I wouldn't have it any other way." His finger touched the edge of her chin. "You can't say I'm not involved. And you can't say you dragged me into this. I came of my own free will."

"I. . .know that. It's just that I can't help worrying over what might happen."

"Our God is bigger than anything that could happen to either of us," Jake replied. "Is that why you've always kept your distance and wouldn't let me get close to you. . .because of vague possibilities."

"They're not vague!" she insisted, backing away. "You saw what happened at the airport. Do you have any idea what it's like to always have someone snooping to catch the latest tidbit? Or worrying that you're the next reason for a ransom note? It's serious."

"I'm willing to take the chance."

She sighed, grateful resignation coloring the sound. "You've been wonderful. . .and I. . .don't know how to thank you."

"You can walk me to a bird's-eye view of the ocean. Do you know I've never seen the Pacific Ocean before today?"

"Really?" She half disbelieved him. "With all the traveling I know you've done?"

Jake smiled. "Always in an easterly or southerly direction. Do we have time?"

"Before the reading? We should. The lawyer isn't here yet. If everyone is ready and I'm not there, Nan will send someone to find me."

The salt air was cool on Krista's cheeks and a light breeze lifted the ends of her hair. The sun was lowering in the sky, its red gold rays tingeing the tips of the cedars with color and painting dancing reflections on the undulating ocean.

Krista rested her arms on the chill, wrought iron fencing and leaned to look down. Jake followed Krista's lead, circling his arm around her shoulders. Below them waves crashed against the cliff, sending their frothy spray upward. Their power could be felt in the trembling rock that protested beneath their feet.

"Awesome, isn't it?" Jake asked. He drew in a breath of the peculiar odor associated with the sea, full of creatures and churning with life.

"I've never liked the ocean," Krista confessed. "At least not like this."

"Why is that?" Jake asked, adjusting his stance. "I find it fascinating to watch."

After some reflection, Krista's hand stretched out, indicating the struggling waves that searched for a place to spread their burdens before drawing back to seek again.

"It's never quiet," she said, "or peaceful. It's always striving, each wave fighting the other for its place and none quite succeeding." She was silent. "Perhaps it's the 'none quite succeeding' that bothers me the most. Or the restlessness of it. I don't know," she said and shook her head, staring at the roiling waves and rocks beneath them.

They were silent, studying the scene below. A thought came to mind and was half spoken before Krista realized it.

"I was going to jump from here once." She felt Jake's reaction—a slight tightening of his grip. The sun was descending beyond the horizon. She squinted against the glare. The water churned and fought below them, shooting spray skyward. "But something stopped me. I couldn't do it. As much as I wanted to just end it all, some. . .weakness. . .kept me from it. I just couldn't jump."

"There is no weakness in standing up and facing life." Jake's voice was quiet and close to her ear. "There's more strength involved with confronting reality than in giving in and saying you can't take it anymore."

"That's easy for you to say," Krista replied. "How could you understand such great despair that you thought you just couldn't face another moment? . . .That life was more than you could endure? I can't imagine you getting to the point where you'd think about ending your life."

Jake was silent. So silent that Krista glanced back in surprise at the man that held her so close. . .and knew she had come to lean on him more than she had realized.

"Have you?" she asked slowly.

"Would that surprise you?"

Krista's mouth slowly dropped. "But you. . ."

". . .Are just a man, like you are just a woman."

"But you have. . .something I've never had—an inner strength. I could never imagine you wanting to. . .to stop living."

"That's because you've seen only two years of my life. Believe me, I haven't always been this way. Let me tell you what is not a secret to many who have known me longer than you." Jake pulled her closer into the shelter of his arms, and Krista permitted herself to be drawn in, with her back against him.

"I haven't always been the way that I am now. My parents are good, loving Christians who taught all their children the best they knew. They were moral, upright, and tried to teach us to trust in Christ and rely on Him to guide and direct our lives."

Krista thought she heard a whispered sigh tickle her cheek.

"But I didn't want to listen. I was going out to conquer the world in my own strength. Except my strength was weak, and it got me in deeper and deeper." Jake hesitated for a moment. "In college," he continued, "I was suddenly free from restrictions. I decided I wanted to experiment. I got into drugs, a common enough story. However, I didn't just take drugs, I hooked other kids, too." He paused and took a breath, his voice deepening as his words began to draw out. "Inside I knew what I was doing was wrong, but the wretchedness of this world sucked me in. . .until the night I watched my best friend go into convulsions from an overdose." Jake tightened his grip on Krista, and she responded by taking hold of his hands and wrapping them with her own fingers.

"Derek died in my arms."

"Oh, *Jake*," Krista whispered and turned in his arms to gaze up at him.

His piney-green eyes flashed at her. "I didn't just consider suicide—I tried it."

Krista's breath drew in sharply.

"A week after Derek died, in a fit of despair, *I* took an overdose. Darrell found me in my apartment and rushed me to the hospital. The doctors didn't have much hope for me. They told me later I was pretty far gone. But Darrell had more faith than all the doctors."

"And you survived," her words came out with thanksgiving. "Were you glad Darrell found you?"

"I hated him."

Krista's grey eyes widened at the impact of his words.

Jake said, "Darrell kept me from escaping this world and all the things I didn't want to think about, but," Jake's voice and expression softened, "he kept talking to me about not being ready to die. He's always had a tough sort of love for me and told me if I wanted to do myself in, then I was free to do it, so long as he knew I was sincerely ready to accept the consequences of death.

"Darrell re-explained to me what I had heard all my life: That when I died there would be a reckoning. I would stand before God and be judged for all the wrong things I've done. Even though I hadn't physically given Derek those drugs, I was still responsible. Yet, I also knew that nothing I could do would put me right with God—that only He could take care of all the disasters I'd created in my life.

"You see," Jake continued, "even though I had heard the gospel all my life, had been raised in church and a Christian home, I had never accepted Jesus Christ as my Savior. I was holding back what God wanted most. I needed to yield to his ability to make me what I needed to be. That night I accepted Christ as Savior and Lord. God gave me His Son, and I accepted that free gift. In return, I needed to allow God to shape the life His Son died for."

"You make it sound so simple."

"It is simple. . .but, also, very difficult. I think, in some ways, that was the hardest time of my life, to realize that I was nothing without God guiding my steps. I'd always been fiercely independent. Yet, too, it was a relief to be able to give in and put all my burdens on Someone else's shoulders. I'd made a mess of things. Perhaps Derek would be alive today if I had been a Christian."

Krista could feel Jake watching her. What he said made sense. To just let go and hand everything over to God. It was easy. . .almost too easy, a small part of her said. Yet, she wanted something more than knowing where she would spend eternity. There was a yearning in her that desired the subtle difference Jake had.

Krista sighed, a weary, curious sound that somehow mimicked her present, peculiar feelings.

"Do you mind if we walk?" she asked.

"Of course not," Jake replied, not pursuing further discussion. . .which relieved Krista. She wanted—needed— time to think.

"Why don't you show me Mariano Estate?" Jake suggested.

"That's quite an order." Krista fell into step with Jake, then tipped her chin toward him, her eyes holding a glint of amusement. "Do you want to see the stables? Or the pools?" One brow tilted upward. "The rifle range? There're also the libraries if you feel in the literary mood. Or perhaps you would rather view some of Uncle Anthony's collections." Both eyebrows shifted upward. "The grounds? There's not much light left," she shrugged, indicating the loss of sunlight, "but Uncle Anthony's gardeners are the finest, and what you will see are some of the best examples of local flora."

Jake grinned and tucked her arm securely into his. "I think. . . the beach."

Krista smiled and forced aside the frustrating sensation that plagued her, of not being totally right in her walk before God or understanding all she needed to understand. Could it be that God was truly interested in everything in her life? Observing the man walking beside her, Krista mentally shook her head at the wonder of it.

Having found a spot sheltered somewhat by a jut of rock, the two of them sat on the sand. It was dusk, the pale grey deepening by the minute. A gull dipped and screeched above them, bringing others of his kind swooping in expectation.

Jake sat crosslegged, face lifted toward the water, letting the sea breeze envelop him. His hands leisurely dribbled sand from between his fingers. Indicating a spot down the beach, Jake asked, "A guest?"

A man and a dog were making their way toward them. After watching his progress for several minutes, they heard the man give a sharp command to his animal and the two of them veered back the way they had come.

"It was a security guard," Krista supplied as explanation. "He won't bother us." Frowning at her thoughts, Krista said, "I don't want to live life trusting bodyguards to insure my privacy—or my safety."

"You won't have to."

"Colorado was nice."

"Krista. . ."

Jake reached over and took her hand. Krista felt the pressure of his arm, the way his fingers caressed, then intertwined with hers. She looked up at him and studied the shape of his face in the failing light—lean, tan, serious. The line of his jaw was raspy-smooth under the tip of her finger as Krista reached to touch him. . .as if to reassure herself that he was truly there, beside her, holding her. A seagull cried as if far away and. . .

"We'll have to leave soon," Jake said softly. "People are probably looking for us."

Us.

"They'll find us if they need us."

. . .He was going to kiss her.

"What are you smiling about?" Jake asked, his face inches from hers, a trace of a grin playing at the corners of his eyes and touching the edges of his lips.

Krista's heart thudded in expectation.

"Nothing. . ."

His eyes were as dark as Colorado pines. . .and his lips slowly moved toward hers. Krista's lashes drooped to her cheeks and she returned the light pressure of his touch. . .a whisper soft caress. His hand touched the side of her cheek, his fingers light and gentle.

"Krista," Jake whispered. "I love you."

—21—

Krista's heart beat rapidly as she stared back at Jake and, unexpectedly, her eyes began to slowly fill with tears. She blinked them back and swallowed the tight ball in her throat.

Jake drew her close to him and Krista let herself be held. One tear escaped and slowly trickled across her face to find a resting place among the tangled threads of her hair. Another followed...and Krista quietly wept away some of her pain and uncertainties.

Minutes passed. The sky darkened. Fog lent its damp chill to the air.

Krista sniffed and wiped at the moisture that lingered on her face. "We should go back," she said.

"When you're ready," Jake replied.

"I'm ready," she said. "It's time to face what needs to be done."

They walked back to the house in silence.

"Thank you...for being with me," Krista said as they paused at the back entrance to the mansion.

Krista could feel the intensity of his gaze through the darkness. His hand touched the side of her face and she felt his lips press against her forehead. "You're welcome."

A servant was standing in the hall with the message. "Mr. Mariano and Miss Carr are waiting for you in the study, Miss Johnston. You are requested to come as soon as it is convenient."

"This is it," Jake said, adding a small twist to his lips.

With a silent look at Jake, Krista led the way to Anthony Mariano's study where a subdued murmur could be heard filtering into the hallway.

Krista stopped at the door and turned to Jake. "I'm. . . scared."

"You'll do fine." He added a reassuring smile and flicked a grain of sand from her cheek, then opened the door.

Steven was seated with Linda to his right and in front of the desk. Mr. Wood, attorney-at-law, reigned in Anthony Mariano's place. The sight of him gave Krista a momentary shock, and she had to remind herself that her uncle would never sit behind that desk again.

In reality it was. . .her place.

Her own lawyer, Mr. Canterbury, had taken a seat to the side, but close to the front of the room. Nan was in a chair to the left and forward of the desk, her hands folded about a handkerchief in her lap. There were a number of others seated nearby or discreetly standing to the side.

The whispers stopped, and as if by common agreement, they all turned to look at her.

One of the servants moved to place another chair for Jake next to Krista.

Krista looked about her. No one resumed talking, they just waited, and it gave her an eerie feeling of their expectations.

Her lawyer glanced her direction and gave a barely discernible nod of his head. Anthony Mariano's lawyer cleared his throat and rustled a stack of papers on the desk before him, then shifted his glasses up his nose and peered at the people around him.

"You all know why you are here," Mr. Wood began. "Each of you, in one way or another, has been mentioned in the late Anthony Alexander Mariano's will. You are here for the reading of that will and the dispensing of his worldly goods."

Krista felt the subtle glances being cast her way. Jake's hand touched hers and gave a light squeeze.

Through the legal jargon came the dispensing of grants, contributions, and donations to worthy causes, and the instructions concerning them. The list was endless and Steven began to fidget. Krista noted Nan's unobtrusive look of disapproval. Linda's hand on Steven's arm stilled him momentarily.

Several household employees were mentioned and sizable awards given to the most loyal and fervent, including a handful of people who were not present in the room. Nan, as yet, had not been mentioned, and Krista was mildly surprised when the servants were given permission to return to their duties, but Miss Carr requested to stay.

There was a brief interlude as the servants departed, their steps muffled on the thick carpeting. In the silence, the soft whisper of their movements was loud and vaguely irritating. Krista yearned for the formality of it all to be done.

"You all know," Mr. Wood said after the last person exited, "that Mr. Mariano was a shrewd businessman. Yet, he was also very generous. He requested that the next portion be read only in the presence of the immediate family, their chosen guests," he conceded Linda and Jake's presence with a nod of his head, "and Miss Carr."

Steven stared at Nan, distrust and misgiving plainly written across his features. Krista watched the interplay between the two and noted the light flush that appeared on Nan's cheeks as her look encountered Steven's, then Krista's before dropping to study her handkerchief for a brief moment before she looked up again at Mr. Wood.

Krista glanced at Jake. Her minute shrug was barely perceptible.

" 'To Miss Nannine Evelyn Carr'," Mr. Wood quoted, " 'I bequeath the amount of one million dollars'," a strangled sound came from Steven's throat, and Krista could not contain her own small draw of breath, " 'to be used as she sees fit, in appreciation for her loyalty to myself and my household over her years of constant service.' Included in that," Mr. Wood continued as his eyes rose to focus on the housekeeper, "is a personal letter which I have here." He held up a cream colored envelope which he handed to Krista's lawyer to pass to Nan. "It's a hefty sum, Miss Carr, but Mr. Mariano stipulated that you were worthy of it. Also instructed is the permanence of your position here at Mariano Estate until such time as you choose to terminate it. You would retain the same responsibilities and privileges as you currently hold."

Nan's acknowledgment of his words was a choked whisper. She had begun to weep silently, the fingers of one hand compulsively pressing flat the padded envelope that lay in her lap.

Mr. Wood returned to the will. " 'To Steven Creighton Mariano'," Steven leaned forward in expectation, " 'I leave the beachfront home in Malibu, expenses for the upkeep of same home, and a yearly allowance of one hundred thousand dollars. . . .'."

"What?!" the exclamation shot explosively from Steven's lips. He hurtled from his seat to shove himself half across Anthony Mariano's desk. Mr. Wood, unruffled, gravely backed a few inches from Steven's threatening form.

"What are you saying?" Steven demanded. His fist thudded on the mahogany top. "You've made a mistake! That's not near enough!"

The documents were lowered as Mr. Wood focused his attention on the distraught form of the man before him. "It's no mistake, Mr. Mariano. The will is. . ."

Steven purpled. His finger jabbed around toward Nan. "You mean to tell me that this. . .*servant*," he enunciated incredulously, "inherits one million dollars and I'm left with one *tenth* of that?"

Mr. Wood peered over his glasses at Steven. "Mr. Mariano," he said, unperturbed at Steven's demonstration. "If you will please return to your seat, we can finish this and all be on our way."

"Steven, please," Linda entreated, having risen to take hold of his arm.

Steven stared at Linda. His glance shot from one person to the next, resting on Krista with an intensity that had her looking from him to Linda's worried face, then to Jake and, fleetingly, Nan.

"Mr. Mariano. . ." the lawyer repeated with a tip of his head in the direction of Steven's chair.

Giving an exclamation of distaste, Steven shrugged off Linda's hand and threw himself back into his chair. Linda settled quietly beside him.

"As I was saying," Mr. Wood began, " '. . .and a yearly allowance of one hundred thousand dollars for the next ten years, after which time the allowance is to be terminated with the fervent hope that he will have reformed his spendthrift ways. If, at that time, he has shown a profit of at least ten percent in the form of a legal business for no less than three of said ten years, there is to be added to his monies an additional five hundred thousand dollars to assist in promoting said business'."

There was a pause of silence.

"That's all?" Steven asked bitterly.

"There are provisions for your personal belongings, including your three cars and whatever collections you may have. Other than that, and the monies you are currently in possession of, yes, Mr. Mariano, I'm afraid that is all your uncle left you."

"And I suppose," Steven said bitterly, spearing Krista with a look, "that she gets all the rest."

Krista tightened her grip on Jake's hand, and felt him return it.

"That is a simplified way of putting it," Mr. Wood replied, "but basically you are correct."

"That's not fair!" Steven shouted.

Nan straightened. "Be quiet, Steven. Your uncle did it for your best interests."

"Who are you to lecture me?" Steven lashed back. "You just got one million dollars!"

Krista interrupted Steven, "I have something to say about the inheritance that Uncle Anthony left for me—something you all need to hear."

Everyone's attention riveted on Krista. She took a breath and straightened, her chin tilting upward as she faced them.

"I think we can safely say that we all knew what Uncle Anthony had planned for me—the running of his companies, the estate, and whatever else he may have been involved with. I think I can also safely say that you all know how I feel about that."

Krista looked around her, noting Nan's face and Steven's piercing eyes. Linda's eyes were huge, her fingertips covering her pale mouth.

"This morning," Krista addressed the group, "I contacted my lawyer. In the event that Uncle Anthony had indeed done exactly that, above my wishes, assuming in the end that I would submit to it, I wanted to be prepared." She took a breath and another glance at each person in attendance.

"Work has been started to donate the estate and other pieces of property to worthy causes." Steven's eyes widened in self-righteous horror. Nan's hands fluttered to her chest as Krista continued. "The estate is to be a Christian school for girls who have no home and have the need of special services. The businesses will be sold and money put into funds to be used to support this school and various other schools that will be set up. This estate," she said, "will be a beginning example. There will also be other contributions, distributed in whatever way my lawyer and I see fit."

"But. . .*why?*" Steven uttered incredulously, barely able to retain his self-control. His hands trembled with emotion and he rose slowly to stand dazed before her. . .before them all. "How could you? You know I need money. You can't help but know it. Yet you'd give it away. . .to people you don't even know."

"Uncle Anthony has made provision for you, Steven. You knew long before now that the money would run out sometime." She shook her head and addressed the entire room. "I will not have Anthony Mariano's money, businesses, or reputation interfere with my life. Once all the papers are drawn up and signed, I will no longer have any ties to this place or the Mariano reputation. And," she took a deep breath, "I am not the same Krista who fled from here two years ago. A few weeks back," Krista took another deep breath, "I accepted Jesus Christ as my Savior. I want the Mariano millions to be used for Him, for something other than self-indulgent hoarding. This Christian school will be a start."

"You've become a religious fanatic." Nan said in quiet certainty. You would give up," Nan asked, "all your uncle has worked for. . .all he wanted you to have? He wanted you happy and secure."

"Money," Krista refuted Nan, "does not insure happiness and security. You and Uncle Anthony taught me that," she paused and allowed her eyes to flick past Jake's silently approving face, "when you proved you could buy off Broderick."

"And if money is what you're most concerned about, you know that I am not destitute. My parents were far from poor when they died. . .and Uncle Anthony invested my parents' inheritance well as I grew up. Why should I want more? So I can make more? Have more things?"

"The Mariano honor. . ." Nan continued.

"I would keep it," Steven uttered with dramatic emphasis, ignoring the declaration of Krista's intentions. His hands waved in the air. "The Mariano name is a proud name."

"Names are what you make of them," Krista answered with a pointed glance.

Steven's jaw tightened as his fingers twisted into fists.

"Have you signed any papers yet?" This was Nan.

"Some. I will finalize others when they are ready. You know Uncle Anthony's holdings are numerous. It will take months, maybe a few years, as much as I hate to admit it, to complete everything. I would hope," Krista inserted with a slight pause for the housekeeper, "that you might consider staying here, Nan, helping the new administrators of the school understand the workings of the estate."

"To have this home taken over by girls. . .of questionable backgrounds. . ." Nan murmured.

Steven uttered, "It won't happen!"

"It's already begun," Krista reminded him. She turned her attention to her lawyer and eased her grip on Jake's hand. "I am correct in what I'm saying, aren't I?"

He nodded in affirmation to her question.

Krista turned her attention to Anthony Mariano's lawyer. "Is there anything more I need to stay for now?"

"There's little more that, at the present, will affect the outcome. I do require your signature on several items," the man replied. "Afterward, much of the remainder can be handled between your lawyer and myself."

"Then let's do it," Krista said, rising from her chair. "I plan to leave for Colorado in the morning if that's possible."

Mr. Wood nodded. "We can arrange whatever is necessary around whatever you plan."

"I appreciate that. I have a job," her eyes met Jake's, which were a sober piney-green, ". . .that requires my presence as soon as possible."

Steven gave a disgusted utterance, and stormed from the room.

Linda, her face sadly apologetic, hesitated before Krista,

then hurried after Steven.

Nan clutched the envelope she had been given and rose slowly from her seat.

"With your permission, Krista, I will go to my quarters."

Krista gazed at her former disciplinarian. "You don't have to ask my permission, Nan. Until you've made your decision about staying at the estate, you are a free agent to do as you wish. You can certainly afford to," Krista's perplexity over Uncle Anthony's extreme generosity colored her voice. "Even then, should you decide to stay, I won't be your mistress for long."

"We will require," Mr. Wood interjected, "your signature on various items, also, Miss Carr. That can be done at a later time, if you prefer."

Nan managed a nod of her head. "Thank you, Mr. Wood. Tomorrow, if you don't mind." She left through the same door as Steven and Linda.

Jake remained seated, a quiet observer to all that was going on.

"So, Mr. Wood. . .Mr. Canterbury," Krista brought her hands together, "shall we get on with it."

Mr. Wood righted the papers in front of him and produced a number to be signed. There were several, also, from Mr. Canterbury, and the process of getting them in order with proper signatures took longer that Krista had anticipated. But, eventually, it was accomplished and both lawyers were straightening and replacing their respective documents in their briefcases.

"If you don't mind my saying so, Krista," Mr. Wood commented with the familiarity of many years acquaintance as he rose from the desk, "I think this is a rather foolish thing you have done. . .but perhaps a bit gutsy, too." His hand came out to connect with hers in a firm shake. "I wish you the very best, Miss Johnston," he said with a smile. "The very best." His head shook in slight wonder as he acknowledged her, then

Jake, and took his leave. Mr. Canterbury mimicked his predecessor, then followed him out the door.

Krista turned to face Jake who was sitting in his chair, elbows resting on the arms and fingertips steepled before him. As they stared at each other, a spurt of fear surged through Krista for an instant before his face began to slowly break into an incredulous grin. His fingers came apart and, hands pressed on the arms of the chair, he stood upright.

"Brilliant," Jake announced. "Utterly brilliant. I never dreamed you would give it all away." His arms came out to encircle her and draw her close. "You are fantastic; do you realize that? Do you realize how many unfortunate peoples' lives will be changed because of you? How many lives may be reached for Jesus Christ? Fantastic," he repeated again. "You are something else."

Krista's grey eyes were wide and shining with pleasure. "Then you're not. . .displeased with me."

"No way. I couldn't be more happy for you." He shifted his grip to allow an arm to remain draped around her. "What do you say. . ." his gaze swept their surroundings, "we get out of here? Let's celebrate!"

Krista's face broke into a delighted smile. "Celebrate?" she asked and laughed. "I give away a king's ransom, have Nan upset, Steven fit to be tied, lawyers shaking their heads at me, and you want to celebrate?" She laughed again. "Lets! What do you want to do?"

"It probably wouldn't be wise to go into town." His nose wrinkled and he shook his head. "Nah, we couldn't do that." Jake's eyes rolled skyward in a show of contemplation. "Basketball isn't very romantic," his index finger thrust upward as he came to an acceptable thought, "so how about a late night swim? If my clothes have arrived. Afterward we could relish my forfeited cup of coffee, a bite to eat, and a cozy corner to talk in. How does that sound, Miss Johnston?"

147

"That sounds like an enjoyable pursuit, Mr. McIntyre."

Jake's clothes had arrived, they discovered as they passed his suite. The ornate furnishings of his room were dressed in variegated shades of blue and gold, and wood had been laid in the fireplace, ready to be started with a touch of a match. The clothes had been hung or placed in drawers and his suitcases put away in the closet.

"Efficient," Jake commented wryly.

"Frustratingly so at times," Krista said.

"That looks like a cheery idea," Jake commented, noting the fireplace.

"The house does have a tendency to get cool in the evening, even in the summer. The fireplace is especially nice after a swim," she added.

"Perhaps we should try that for ourselves, then. Come on; I'll walk you to your rooms so you can change."

Jake and Krista traversed the short distance down the hall. At her door she said, "I'll just take a few minutes to change."

Jake agreed, his eyes flashing. "I'll be back in five minutes."

Krista turned to open her door, but found herself being drawn back into Jake's arms. She thrilled to his brief kiss. "I'll make it three," he said softly.

A surge of happiness ran through Krista. Jake released her and left to hurry down the hall.

Just as Krista reached to open her door, it swung inward, away from her touch. Nan was leaving, her arms ladened with the tray of unused cups and pot of coffee.

"I thought I would remove it," she explained as she stood aside to permit Krista's entrance.

"I understood you were going to your quarters."

"I changed my mind. I prefer to be busy. I think better when I am working. Will you want this replaced?" she asked, slightly lifting the tray.

"Later," Krista answered, studying Nan. "I would like a meal sent up for Mr. McIntyre and myself, but we plan to do some swimming first."

"I will see that it is taken care of."

"Thank you." Then, "Nan. . .does this mean you plan to stay on here at the estate?"

"I am giving it some consideration," she admitted, then left.

Krista watched the housekeeper go, a slight frown knotting her forehead. She shook her head, not knowing what to think, then promptly turned her thoughts aside.

Quickly changing into her swimsuit, Krista pulled a long sweatshirt on over it. As she flicked a brush quickly through her hair, she heard Jake call her name.

"Coming," Krista raised her voice in answer. Opening the door, she waved him inside, then scurried to grab a plush pink towel from the bathroom.

Jake was on the telephone when she re-entered the living room, and he smiled as he raised a finger to hold her attention, then crooked it toward himself. He was wearing sandals and a short terry jacket over his long swimming trunks. Krista went willingly to him, tangling her fingers with his when his hand reached for her.

"No. . .everything is fine," Jake was saying. "Krista's getting things settled here, and she wants to come home tomorrow. I think that's a great idea." She caught his open, happy gaze. "How's the night going?" he asked. Krista strained to listen but was unable to decipher Darrell's, comments. "Good," Jake said. "Great. Well, I'm off for a late night swim with a lovely lady." There was a pause and Jake laughed. "We'll be home real soon," Jake said, "then we'll discuss it."

"Discuss what?" Krista asked as Jake hung up the telephone.

"Wouldn't you like to know?" Jake replied, then his grin turned to a slight frown as his focus shifted from Krista.

"Did you see those?"

"See what?"

"Those," Jake said and moved toward the fireplace mantel where he lifted two small envelopes propped against. . . .

"My billfold!" Krista squealed and snatched it. "How? Who?" Then, "Why didn't Nan say anything? She was here." She added at Jake's look, "when I came into the room. She was removing the coffee tray. I would think she'd have noticed the billfold. Maybe not, though. She seemed preoccupied."

Studying the square, white envelopes, a faint trepidation traced skeleton fingers over Krista's nerves. She fought it. After all, what did she have to worry about now? Yet. . .it had to have been returned by someone who knew who she was. . . which left very few people other than herself and Jake. She slid her finger under the tucked flap of the first envelope.

Dear Krista,

I'm sorry I have to leave without seeing you. Broderick found your billfold, but I talked him into letting me be the one to return it. I'll be in touch.

With fondest regards,
Jennifer

Krista handed the note to Jake and opened the other envelope.

Don't think it's over.

150

—22—

The second note was signed with a forcefully scrawled B.

Wordlessly, Krista handed it to Jake.

After a moment's hesitation, Krista spoke. "He's like this," she said. "He doesn't know what it means to give up. Even if he did let Jennifer return my billfold, it doesn't mean he didn't stop to record my address." Her hand came out with a weary, defeated wave of the billfold. "This is what I was afraid of. It'll never be over, Jake, never."

Silently, Jake dropped the envelopes and notes next to the telephone. He took the billfold from Krista's grasp and placed it there, also.

Folding her hands to his chest, Jake captured her gaze. "We're going for a swim," he said. "After that we can think about filling my starving midsection."

Krista's eyes flicked from the pile on the end table back to Jake. She wavered between her worries and Jake's determination to not permit Broderick to ruin their evening. Her head tilted. Krista studied the man who held her. Slowly her mouth crooked with a determined smile. She turned her back on the troublesome envelopes and led the way to the pool.

A large glass door, one of many leading to the pool, whooshed into place behind them and latched shut.

The pool was serene, with light ripples reflecting the translucent quality of the water's surface. Small table and chair groupings were placed strategically against the corners and along the walls, some secluded, others convenient for watching the pool. Krista and Jake were alone.

The vast, empty room was enveloped by an echoing silence that slightly unnerved Krista. She and Jake made their way to poolside where Krista kicked off her sandals and looked about her. She hugged her arms to herself, feeling dwarfed by the size of the room. . .and her emotions. So many hours she had spent in this room, studying, perfecting her swimming and diving technique. . . .

"I always wanted to whisper when I was the only one using the pool," Krista admitted to Jake. "It's so big. . .and so. . . empty."

Jake's grin broke into mischievous delight.

"Not for long!" he replied.

Krista shrieked. Jake swung his arm under her legs and lifted. Krista's cry went to laughter, then another squeal as he unceremoniously dumped her, sweatshirt, towel, and all into the deep end.

Krista swirled, her legs and arms momentarily fighting the resistance of her surroundings. Then she relaxed, and shot to the surface.

Jake grinned impishly.

"Are you all wet?" he asked, dropping his jacket beside his sandals.

Krista gave a kick and floated to the side. Her towel scattered shining droplets of water as it arced out of the water and slapped on the tile floor.

"Give me a hand up? This sweatshirt weighs a ton."

"Sure." Jake smiled and reached down to grasp her wrist.

Snatching his arm, Krista braced her feet against the side of the pool and tugged as hard as she could. . .only to lurch backward with another squeal of defeat.

Krista splashed to the surface and wiped water from her eyes.

Jake was shaking his head, the glint of roguery in his eyes

contradicting the forlorn look on his face. "I must have lost my grip," he said teasingly.

Krista swam to the edge and levered herself up to sit on the side. Her sweatshirt draped heavily about her shoulders and, as she stood, loosed its captured water, hanging nearly to her knees.

Jake gave a small leap and sliced the water with a neat dive, popping to the surface several yards away.

"How fast are you?" he asked, pointing a quick jab toward the far end of the pool.

"Fast enough," Krista replied, as she struggled to peel the layer of cotton fleece over her head and off her arms.

"Come on."

The garment dropped with a splat at her feet.

"You have the advantage." Krista studied her opponent, hands on hips, debating her chances of actually beating him in a race. "You're already fifteen feet on your way to the finish line."

Jake moved toward her.

"I'll give you a head start."

"All right."

Krista's dive cut the water cleanly. It had been years since she had trained for speed and endurance, months since she had been in a pool. Still, she was in shape, and the action came as naturally as if she had been swimming the day before.

She was a strong swimmer, but she could sense Jake gaining on her. . .in spite of her advantage.

Krista's hand touched the side of the pool; she sucked in a breath and stood upright in the four foot depth.

"You're fast," she gasped.

"You're not too shabby yourself."

"Did you neglect to tell me something?"

He smiled. "Like. . .the fact that I was on the swim team in college?"

"Something like that." She tilted her head back and washed the hair out of her eyes, smoothing it with her hands.

"Did you dive, too?" Krista asked, accepting his hand up. She settled beside him on the tiled edge.

"No. I left that to the more dedicated. Of course, . . ." his eyes became vaguely shadowed, ". . .other things interfered with what I might have done."

Krista touched his arm. "I shouldn't have brought it up. . . ."

Jake's smile was immediate. "It was part of my life. But now it's over and in the past. . .just like this," his gaze scanned their surroundings, "will be for you someday. You will leave behind memories of here just as I left behind memories of my college days."

A touch of a frown creased Krista's brow. She kicked the water with her feet, feeling it swirl about her calves and between her toes.

It would not, she realized, be an easy task to leave behind all the hurt and pain of what it meant to be a Mariano—the realization that people cared for her only because of her uncle's money. All they could see was the vast wealth and the power behind it, not who she really was as a person.

Krista thought back to their earlier conversations, considering the person beside her. . .who he was and why.

"Was it really God working in your life that made the difference, Jake?"

"Yes."

Krista looked at him. His reply had been instantaneous, without hesitation. She said, "I've seen your Bible on your desk at work. . .and I know you pray a lot—even when people might see. You go to church almost every Sunday, and your family cares about each other. . .in a way I've never encountered before."

"Those things are a part of my life, yes, but they're not what makes my relationship with God work."

Krista scrutinized the man beside her. "What. . .does make it work, Jake?"

"First of all, the sure knowledge of my forgiveness through God's Son, Jesus. Without that I could not have found the strength to forgive myself. . .to keep on living."

"Jesus and how He died. . .for my sins. . .is what I accepted two months ago. But there's more, isn't there?"

"Yes, there is," Jake replied.

Krista was quiet. "Go on."

"You can take what God has given you—the free gift of His Son—and live however you think is right. It may look okay on the outside, and you may even think you're satisfied with the way things are. Or," Jake studied Krista, "you can acknowledge God as the Lord of your life, strive to please Him. . .and discover the blessing of living for God."

Krista hesitated. "The thought of. . .just giving in is hard for me to do," she said. "I've given in all of my life—to Uncle Anthony, to Nan, even to Steven and. . .Broderick. For the past two years I've been able to be free of that. I've been able to be *me*, Jake—not what someone else wants me to be."

Jake was silent for a moment. "I won't tell you that God doesn't try to change you, Krista. He does. He wants us to grow daily in a closer walk with Him. To become more and more Christ-like. I praise God that He did change me. I couldn't have lived with the man I was before I accepted Christ as Lord of my life. You wouldn't have liked me very much, either."

Krista faced him in surprise.

Jake's head nodded solemnly.

"I was a nasty, self-centered, ruthless person, hard as it may seem to you to believe," he replied at the look of denial in Krista's grey eyes. "There wasn't anything I wouldn't have done to get my own way. You wouldn't want to hear the half of what I've done. . .and I'd hate to repeat it."

155

Krista digested this for a moment. She could not imagine Jake being selfish or egotistical or. . .offensive.

"Did the problems in your life get. . .easier. . .once you took that step?" she asked.

Jake thought carefully.

"I can't say that they did. If anything, I think there was a time when everything seemed to fall apart, seemingly worse than it had been before. However," Jake continued, looking directly into Krista's eyes, "that was when I found a strength to rely on that I had never had before. God is that strength. I finally came to the point where I trusted Him completely. He never failed to get me through those tough times. He won't fail you either, Krista. God wants to bless you. And He will as you honor Him and try to obey Him—like you did today."

Water swirled in ever increasing patterns away from Krista's moving legs, stretching to brush the far end. Faintly lapping ripples. She watched them move. Did she believe God would require more than she could give back of herself?

One of the large doors swung open, the noise abnormally loud in the echoing room. A servant hurried careful, whispering steps along the length of the pool and approached Jake and Krista. With the briefest of interruptions, he handed an envelope to Jake and exited by the closest door.

"What is it?" Krista asked as Jake unfolded the slip of paper inside.

"Darrell wants me to contact him. I wonder what the problem is?"

"There's a telephone over here," Krista said, moving to a nearby chair and table grouping where a telephone had been conveniently placed. Jake grabbed his terry cloth jacket and draped it over his shoulders. He lifted the receiver and placed it to his ear.

"Dead," Jake said, glancing with a puzzled look at Krista before replacing the instrument.

"What?" Krista asked, perplexed. "There are others. But,

wait," she stopped and crooked her finger at Jake. "There's a private telephone this way. It was Uncle Anthony's. He used this room whenever private calls came through," she explained. "It saved him the inconvenience of having to return to his study so he wouldn't be overheard."

The door was wooden, with no window. To ensure absolute privacy, Krista also knew it was soundproof. She flicked on the light in the small office. It was neat, and Krista got the impression Uncle Anthony had not used it for quite some time. Jake lifted the telephone receiver and smiled. It worked. He dialed the number for McIntyres'.

"Busy," he said and tried again. "Still busy. Listen," he told Krista, "why don't you go on out and practice a few dives for me? I'd like to see your style before we call it a night. How does that sound?"

Krista smiled. "I'm apt to be rusty even with some practice."

"I doubt it, if your swimming ability says anything about it."

"Flattery," she teased.

"I'll be out in a couple of minutes." Jake punctuated his words with a smile and wave of his hand to shoo her on her way. "Nothing too fancy," he admonished and turned to dial the numbers again.

Krista pushed through the door, allowing it to shut behind her. Around her the air was warm, but the tile floor was cool beneath her feet. She made her way to the high dive.

The thought crossed her mind to practice on the low dive first, but she discarded the thought. She was not that much out of practice, and she didn't plan to do anything elaborate.

Climbing the ladder to the top, Krista tested the spring in the board. She doubted anyone had adjusted it since she left. Pacing her steps to the end of the board, Krista studied the room around her. . .the bright lights, the wiggly lines beneath the surface of the still undulating water. She remembered Broderick's voice giving commands from the poolside, always demanding the best.

Krista gave a light hop and sprang into a tuck.

The lights went out.

Krista struck the water in perfect form, the years of training not affected by her surprise over the sudden darkness. The silence of the water surrounded her, and her sense of equilibrium sent her rising to the surface. Popping through she took a quick breath. She had never realized the room could be so dark.

"Jake. . .?" Her voice was a whispering question that filled the empty room.

A flashlight flicked on close to the edge. Krista could make out a vague figure behind it.

"Thank goodness," she said, making her way to the side. "I can't imagine what happened. The lights never fail this time of year. Why haven't the generators taken over?" she wondered aloud, reaching to pull herself out of the water.

A hint of movement startled her. Something was terribly wrong. She threw herself backward. . .too late. A hard blow struck the side of her head.

Krista dropped into the water, swirling in the inky depths, oblivious to the silence around her.

—23—

Someone was there.

Who?

Where?

Sand. Under her feet. The pounding of waves made the ground tremble and shift and she tried to run, but it was so hard to move.

Jake. Where was Jake?

She hurt.

A noise. Somewhere Jake was calling her name, but she could not find him.

The fog. When had the fog come in? Grey tendrils reached out and grabbed at her, snatching her clothes, pulling her hair.

She tried to scream, but could not. Fear gripped her.

Jake. Where was Jake? She had to find Jake.

She was tired. So very tired.

A noise. A voice.

She concentrated.

The fog was thick. She pushed at its swirling form.

Hands grabbed at her, pushing, forceful, a voice urgent in her ear.

Krista gasped. Coughed. Wretched.

"Thank God!" she heard.

Jake.

Krista wretched again and whimpered his name.

"It's all right. I'm here," he assured her, drawing her into his arms.

There were lights. She frowned against the glare. . .and the throbbing pain in her head.

Jake was wet. The curls of his blond hair were dark and plastered to his head. His eyes were wide, his face twisted.

There were servants. Anxious voices. People. A security guard.

Jake pushed a soft towel across her mouth, her face, brushing back her hair, wiping away the water.

Krista whispered, "The lights. . ."

The security guard spoke. "Someone tripped a main switch."

"Thank God the lights in the office still worked," Jake uttered. "I called for help. . .found a flashlight."

"S-someone. . .*hit me.*" Krista had begun to tremble, her body quivering with uncontrollable shaking.

"Shock," she heard someone say.

"Call an ambulance," Jake ordered.

"*No!*" The word tore from her throat. "No. P-please!" she cried. "No h-hospital. F-find Nan. . ."

"I'm here, child."

Krista saw the housekeeper's face, breathless, bent low, close to hers. "T-tell them," she whimpered. "No h-hospital."

"I'll call Dr. Lowery," Nan assured her, then said to Jake, "We must get her to her room."

Someone wrapped a blanket around her. Jake lifted her into his arms. She buried her face in his neck.

She knew she was moving, but lost all sense of direction. Nor did she care. Her head hurt. She shuddered and Jake held her close.

Nan was giving Jake quietly terse directions, scurrying ahead to open doors, pull down the covers of her bed, draw the draperies. She gave orders for another servant to call Dr. Lowery, then left briefly when the servant had the doctor on the line.

Jake remained next to her bed, holding her hand, talking to her, brushing her hair back from her face.

"S-someone h-hit me."

Jake was shushing her, but she insisted, her hand reaching up to touch the ache on the side of her skull.

"He. . .hit me."

"*Hit you?*" Jake's face became a study of conflicting emotions as Krista's words made an impact. "What are you talking about? Who hit you?"

Who? Broderick? She frowned. A sense of horror overcame her. *Steven?*

"I. . .couldn't see."

Nan re-entered the room.

"Mr. McIntyre," the housekeeper said calmly. "If you would please give us a few moments? The doctor is on his way, and Krista will need to get out of those wet things."

Krista clutched Jake's hand tighter.

Jake lifted Krista's hand to his lips and touched the back of her fingers softly. The light in his eyes softened to loving gentleness.

"Just for a short time," he said. "I'll come back as soon as Miss Carr is done. I'll just be right outside your door. I won't go any further, I promise."

Releasing his fingers reluctantly, Krista submitted. She watched him pass through the doorway and close the door behind him, the doorknob slowly twisting back into place as he released his grip on the other side.

Krista stared at Nan.

Why would someone do this to me? she wondered.

Nan's hands were efficient, as always.

Was it Steven?

Krista could almost predict Nan's actions as she drew warm clothes from the chest of drawers.

Broderick?

161

The sweatshirt was warm and soft, the jeans felt wonderful against Krista's skin.

Why?

"I smell like chlorine."

The comment came from somewhere—a grasp at reality. Reality was not, could not be, someone trying to kill her.

"At least you can still smell," Nan replied quietly. "What happened? I could not make much sense of anything at the pool."

Krista's eyes sharpened on the woman who now pressed her down on the bed. Krista's voice was surprisingly strong.

"Someone shut off the lights and. . .hit me."

Krista frowned, shifting her body uncomfortably at the memory. The lights, the flashlight, the blow. She flinched, her face twisting. "I think he was trying. . .to kill me."

Nan stared at Krista. "Who would want to do such a thing?"

"I don't know. . .but I have an idea."

Nan paled. "Who?"

Krista shook her head. A mistake. Her eyes closed against the pain, and she lifted her hands to lay the palms on either side of her pounding skull.

She would make no accusations. She had no proof.

"Please ask Mr. McIntyre to come back in."

Nan did as Krista requested, then brought a chair for Jake to sit on.

Jake and Krista studied one another. Someone had retrieved a shirt and pair of jeans for him. Krista could see the questions written on his face, but she was at a loss to explain anything more than what he already knew. Except for his own confirmation of a possibility or two, there was nothing definite.

Jake brushed drying strands of hair back from her cheek. It was a gentle, tickling sensation that made her heart swell with appreciation for him. His fingers laced with hers.

Jake said softly, "The doctor should be here soon."

Krista's grey eyes studied the way his lips moved. The way his brow could dip, yet raise at the same time so that she could read a dozen expressions in one look.

"I love you, Jake."

He smiled lovingly back at Krista's still form. "I've been waiting for weeks to hear those words from you."

"I want to go home."

"I'll take you there as soon as the doctor gives us the okay to leave." He hesitated, then said. "I think we should call the police."

Nan's breath drew in sharply, quietly.

"No," Krista said.

"This is serious. Someone tried to hurt you. . .to. . .*kill* you."

"Why?" Nan interjected. "Who could possibly want to harm Krista?

"Are you certain you couldn't see who it was?" Jake asked.

Krista grimaced as she struggled with her thoughts.

"It all happened so quickly. It was so dark. . .and he stood behind a flashlight. I just couldn't see clearly."

There was a light tap on the door, and Nan moved to open it.

Dr. Lowery was an older, tall, congenial man with a fatigued look about his lean face. The Mariano family had used his services for many years. Starting with a spat of direct questioning, his examination was brief, but thorough, and he did not hesitate to tell Krista that, "My preference is to admit you to the hospital for the night for observation. I'd like some x-rays to make certain you don't have a concussion."

"I won't go," Krista announced.

There was a small sigh from the doctor. "It's not as if I didn't expect you to say that. You've always had a stubborn streak

163

about my hospital, young lady." He raised his eyes toward where Jake stood. "Talk some sense into her?"

"I'm sorry, Dr. Lowery, but he can't," Krista answered before Jake could reply. Jake had been about to agree with Dr. Lowery. She ignored his look. "Besides, my head doesn't hurt as much as it did before you got here, and I intend to leave tomorrow morning."

Dr. Lowery gave twisted, lop-sided grimace of a grin and began replacing instruments into his bag. "Aspirin should help ease any discomfort. You know what to watch for," he added and redirected his attention toward Nan and Jake. "Nausea, dizziness, disorientation. I would suggest," he returned his attention to Krista, "that if you do leave tomorrow, that you consult your doctor wherever you are going and have another checkup. . .just to make certain that there are no delayed reactions." He paused in his movements. "You aren't planning a strenuous vacation, are you?"

"I'm going back to work," Krista replied.

Dr. Lowery's entire face shifted. His surprised glance flicked toward Nan, on to Jake, then back to Krista. "I'd suggest you take it easy for a few days, at least."

"She will, Doctor," Jake assured him. "I'll see to that." His voice allowed for no argument.

"Yes, well," Dr. Lowery gripped his case and observed his patient. "You listen to this young man and be careful with yourself."

"I will," Krista replied.

Dr. Lowery planted a smile on his weary face, patted Krista's shoulder and left with assurances that he could find his own way out.

Nan located aspirin in Krista's bathroom and gave her a small glass of water. Swallowing them, Krista heaved a sigh and levered herself upright.

Nan uttered an immediate, uncharacteristic, squawk of disapproval. "You must not get up," she said. "You need to

164

rest." Her head shook. "I really feel you should reconsider leaving tomorrow. This job of yours can certainly wait an extra day or two. If you must rest anyway, you may as well stay here."

"Excuse me," Krista said and reached for Jake's hand.

"You *are* a stubborn lady," Jake said in agreement with the doctor's earlier statement. He supported her around the shoulders as she placed her feet on the floor and stood upright.

"Dizzy?" Jake asked.

"No. It just hurts—like a headache."

Nan asked, "Are you serious about leaving in the morning?"

"I have nothing to stay for, no reason to be here."

"You. . .plan to go through with. . .ridding yourself of all your uncle left you."

"Others, more needy than I, will benefit from my decision, Nan." Krista gave the housekeeper her full gaze. Jake slid his arm to her waist. "I'm sorry if my plans offend you, but you've known for years how I felt about accepting the responsibility of the Mariano fortune."

"Would it. . .not be possible for you to allow Steven to take it over if you care so little about what your uncle did for you?"

Steven. Krista frowned mentally, her eyes widened a fraction, then became shadowed with her thoughts.

Krista drew a breath. "Steven has been allotted what Uncle Anthony decided was best for him. Besides, you know as well as I that he would simply gamble it away. How long do you think it might take? One hundred and eighty million dollars worth of holdings?" Krista shook her head. "Perhaps a lifetime, but in the end, there would be nothing."

Nan gave the tiniest sound of resignation, her folded hands lifting once, then dropping before her.

"I may stay on for awhile," Nan said, "until I see how the

transition progresses."

"Of course. You may stay for as long as you choose."

"I will have food sent up," Nan continued, with deference to the earlier wish from her mistress. "Will there be anything else?"

Krista glanced at Jake who was patiently observant to the exchange between her and Nan. He shrugged. "I don't believe so," Krista replied.

Nan made her quietly dignified exit.

Krista heaved a breath, her hand coming up to touch the knot on the side of her head.

Jake asked, "Why won't you inform the authorities?"

"Because it wouldn't do any good. I know you're worried. So am I. I just can't imagine who would try to do something like this to me."

"You said Steven threatened this very thing earlier today."

"Yes, but. . ."

"You have someone else in mind?"

"Broderick?" Her face was puzzled. She paced a few steps, turning with a lift of her hands. "Then there could be any number of Uncle Anthony's associates who have a vendetta against him."

Krista rubbed her cheeks with her palms, as if to wipe away all the disturbing thoughts. Her lips tightened. She wandered to the window and drew back the draperies to gaze out at the darkness. Fog. It gave a surrealistic quality to the trees and grounds. The ocean was a distant, muted rumble. Faint patches of window light produced vague halos on the grounds.

Jake came up behind her to wrap his arms around her waist, accepting her temporary need for silence. Krista laid her arms across his and relished the sensation of being cherished. To know that Jake agreed with her decision to leave Mariano Estate and all it meant to be a Mariano was

166

almost more than she could have hoped for. Darrell was right. Jake was not a gold digger. Her heart swelled with intense joy. She would be grateful to leave in the morning and be done with all of this.

An angry splat struck the outside window ledge.

Krista jerked in surprise.

"What was that?" Jake exclaimed, his arm tightly squeezing her midsection.

A ting preceded a neat hole in the window just to the right of where they stood, with a corresponding smack in the ceiling behind and above them in almost the same instant.

—24—

Krista screamed as Jake whirled her away from the window and flung her to the floor. There was a tink and thunk of another shot. They tumbled as Jake pushed Krista flat against the carpet, the coarse softness pressing into her cheek.

"Don't move!" he ordered and hurriedly crawled back to the window.

"Jake!" Krista screamed.

Jake snatched the lower hem of the heavy draperies and jerked, yanking each panel back into place.

"We're leaving. Now. Stay low," he admonished as Krista rose on her hands and knees to follow his directions. Krista could barely think.

This can't be happening. It isn't possible.

"Krista. . .?" It was a cautious, questioning, feminine voice from the hallway.

Linda.

"S-stay there!" Krista struggled to raise her voice above the fear that threatened to rob her of speech.

"Don't come in," Jake ordered, then asked Krista, "Do you need anything else?"

She tried to think. Her head gave one brief shake.

Jake's hand reached toward her. "Let's get out of here."

Linda, wide-eyed and pale, stood just outside the doorway in her robe, her hair loose about her shoulders.

"What's going on? I heard a scream."

"Where's Steven?" It was a demand from Jake as he slammed the suite door behind himself and Krista. Krista

168

swayed and leaned into him.

Jake repeated his question, and Linda stared at the two of them.

"He. . ." Linda began, "he's not here. He. . .had to go out for awhile. He said he'd be back when he took care of some business."

Krista's look glittered at the young woman before her. "Someone shot at us—through the window."

Linda gasped, a look of horror transforming her features to a pitiful mask. Her entire body began to shake with sudden realization. "You don't really think. . ."

"At this point," Jake inserted, "we don't know what to think, except that someone is trying to kill Krista."

"Steven wouldn't!" Linda besought Krista with a pathetic cry. "You know he couldn't. He's got his faults, but *murder?*"

"You saw him at the reading of the will—and I heard him earlier in the library." Linda paled at Krista's words. "Steven's always been reckless—especially when he's trying to save his own neck."

There was a commotion at the doorway as other people arrived, some fully dressed, others in their nightclothes. A security guard arrived to create some order. Linda moved further into the room, remaining behind when the others dispersed.

The security guard was firing questions about a reported scream.

"Yes, there was a scream," Jake hastened to answer the man as soon as the door shut. "Someone tried to shoot Miss Johnston through her window."

"We heard no gunshots," the guard replied.

Jake responded dryly, "You'll find the bullet holes."

The guard moved toward Krista's bedroom, caution in his stance. He opened the door and asked, "Which one?" as he approached the pair of windows.

"The one on the left," Jake replied from the door. Krista chanced a furtive glance over Jake's shoulder and saw the security guard lift the edge of the draperies. He followed the probable line of impact and glanced around the walls, his eyes drawn toward the ceiling in time to see a small chunk of plaster drop to Krista's vacated bed.

"This will have to be reported to the police," the guard replied.

"Fine. You do that," Jake said, "but, by the time they arrive, Miss Johnston and I will no longer be here. I'm taking her home. If you or the authorities need to ask questions, Miss Carr knows how to get in touch with me."

The man turned back toward the living area, replacing the drapery. "Under the circumstances that's not a very wise idea. . . ."

"I will not permit Miss Johnston to stay here any longer," Jake replied, determination putting steel in his voice. "We are leaving. Krista, do you have your car keys?"

"Over there," she pointed, "in my purse."

Jake strode to where her purse lay and extracted the keys to her sports car. Handing them to the security man, Jake said, "You'll find Miss Johnston's car in the garage. A burgundy, late model sports car. Pull it to the front door within the next five minutes."

The man looked to Krista for verification and she nodded. In deference to who she was, he acquiesced, although it was obvious he disagreed with Jake's decision.

A few curious faces of people lingering in the hallway peered around the guard as he opened and closed the door. Krista could hear him talking with them, assuring them that all was well, and they could go back to their business.

Krista's attention riveted on Linda who had been mutely waiting.

"He didn't do it," the girl said in a strained voice.

"At this point it really doesn't matter much, does it?" Krista answered. "It can't be proven one way or the other."

Jake caught Linda's elbow and steered her in the direction of the door. "No matter what you think you heard, he couldn't!" Linda argued, as Jake encouraged her out the door and pushed it shut briefly.

"Grab what you need," he said, "we're taking off."

Krista's eyes scanned the room. She grabbed her wallet, purse, and jacket. Together, Jake and Krista scurried down the hall, stopping briefly at Jake's room for him to slide his billfold into his back pocket.

"Why bring the car to the front door?" Krista asked as they hurried down the hallway.

"It's not isolated. There will be more light and less chance of anyone taking another pot shot at you."

Pushing open the door to the library balcony, Krista touched a light switch to flood the room below with light. It was empty. They trotted down the stairs and to the door that opened onto the hallway.

Krista could hear voices, low murmurs, in the ballroom. A doorman stood at the front door.

Jake signaled for the man to be quiet and for Krista to wait. The servant was older, one Krista knew, and she raised a finger to her lips to reiterate Jake's unspoken command. The man did not so much as raise an eyebrow. He stood aside.

Jake opened the front door cautiously. Brass lanterns cast their pale light into the gloom. Jake peered into the foggy night, then grabbed Krista's hand and they ran down the steps to her car.

Jake thrust Krista into the passenger side, snatched the keys from the man who was waiting with the car, and started the ignition.

In minutes, the Mariano Estate had been left behind.

Krista glanced across the bay to see a ghostly mirage glowing dimly in the fog. Then Jake turned a corner, and it vanished from sight. She looked at Jake.

Jake's hands gripped the steering wheel. His eyes bored holes in the darkness. She could feel the intensity of his emotions being held in check.

Cautiously, Krista asked, "What do we do now?"

"Go back to Colorado." Jake's voice had a tone in it Krista had never heard before. "Until we can find out who is doing this, you'll have to stay someplace where no one knows where you are. You can't be seen until we know."

They were coming to the on-ramp to the freeway. Abruptly Jake pulled over to the side and parked. He looked at Krista with an encouraging smile and grasped her hand.

"I'm going to pray," Jake said. "Jesus Christ is Lord of our lives. He doesn't allow incidents to happen without a purpose behind them. I don't understand why this is happening, but I still trust and believe Him when he said He would never leave us or forsake us. Also," Jake said, "He would not want me to have the feelings I have right now, and I need to talk to him about that."

"Whatever you say," Krista agreed softly, studying the planes of Jake's features in the glow from the dash lights.

Jake closed his eyes and dipped his head. His hand tightened on Krista's, and she wrapped her free hand over their laced fingers as she closed her eyes.

"Dear Father," Jake said, "all things are in your hands. You know the situation Krista is in right now, and I just ask that you will give me the wisdom to know what to do to protect her. I confess my anger toward the person who is doing this to her. Help me to forgive him, knowing that you will bring all this around for good. In Jesus' name we ask it. Amen."

"Amen," Krista repeated solemnly.

Jake put the car into gear, entered the highway, and gathered speed. Miles swept by in a blur of curves and flashing headlights.

About one hundred and fifty miles south of the estate, Jake

stopped at an all night quick stop for gas, food, and coffee. The two of them ate dry, tough sandwiches and stale chips as they sipped at the hot, black liquid.

Somewhere before reaching the northern San Francisco area and turning east, Krista fell asleep. Odd, disjointed dreams of people pursuing her filled her sleep. They were mazes of confusion, some moments blending with reality and some not. In them all was an unfinished work she needed to do, but try as she might, she could not quite grasp what it was.

Jake stopped periodically for gas, but Krista paid little attention. The stress of the past week had caught up with her, and she was content to let him take care of what needed to be done. Her head no longer hurt as it had, but the dull ache that remained made it easier to go back to sleep than to try to face reality.

Flashes of sunlight filtering through pine trees finally brought Krista to a sleepy awareness. Puzzled, she murmured, "Where are we?" She stretched conservatively in the confines of her seat.

Weary fatigue lines creased Jake's face. He managed a gritty smile and said, "Close to Lake Tahoe. Did you sleep well?"

"I had. . .strange dreams."

"Small wonder," Jake said, not unkindly. "How does your head feel?"

Krista's hand rose to inspect the knot that remained on the side of her skull. "Sensitive," she said, "but not painful anymore."

"Good."

"Do you want me to drive?" Krista asked.

"I'd rather find a place to stop for awhile. I don't think it would be wise for you to drive yet. There's a lodge up ahead. I'm hoping they have some rooms. I've got to get some sleep."

There were two rooms, cancellations by vacationers who had changed their minds at the last minute. Krista saw Jake smile, and she knew what he was thinking: God had provided for their needs.

Her room was small, but neat and clean with rustic features. Jake purchased several magazines for her, plus an odd assortment of toiletries for both of them since neither had brought anything other than what they wore.

Jake was next door, and Krista had the impression that the covers of his bed would not get turned down before he was asleep—that he would sleep fully clothed on top of the spread.

Kicking off her shoes, Krista crawled onto her bed and sat cross-legged, mechanically thumbing through the magazine in front of her. She tossed it away, unable to concentrate on the pictures or articles.

The events of the past week filled her thoughts. So much had happened, so many terrifying things.

A picture of Jake rose unbidden in her mind. Krista shifted her legs and moved her knees up under her chin. She was not really tired, since she had slept the greater portion of the night, but she was uneasy. Questions kept coming to mind and, surprisingly, they revolved around what Jake had said— about Jesus being Lord of his life.

Trust in the Lord with all your heart, and do not lean on your own understanding. In all your ways acknowledge Him, and He will make your paths straight.

Krista frowned, her fingers lightly touching the lump under her hair.

She had certainly made a mess of her life.

She thought of herself and her need—for someone to care and to trust and to help her be who she ought to be. She considered Jake's reliance on God, the way he drew strength from prayer. She thought of his past. . .and the present. She needed that inner confidence—that something greater.

"*God wants to bless you.*" Jake's words sounded in her mind.

All she had to do was acknowledge His Lordship and submit to His plan for her life.

"Oh, God," she whispered, sudden anguish welling in her, "you've brought this man into my life for this purpose, haven't you? To draw me closer to you and show me the depths and fullness of your love." Her glance focused unseeingly on a spot near the ceiling. "Father, thank you for your Son, Jesus; thank you for forgiving my sins, for making me your child. Yet, only you know the emptiness that remains in my heart." Her eyes closed. "Lord, I need you to forgive me for not wanting to give all of my life to you. I need your peace from the unrest and willfulness in my life. Please forgive me for my selfishness. Help me, Lord God, to be willing to do whatever you want. Help me to trust in you and not lean on my own understanding. Take my life and make it what you want me to be. Thank you, Father," she spoke softly, a smile growing through the release of tears that, unbidden and barely noticed, crept down her cheeks, "for giving me Jake, for his testimony and love for you—and for hearing my prayer."

Krista gloried in the release that swept through her; the burden was gone. She rose and paced her small room, awareness etching each detail of the small quarters into her mind.

Turning, Krista faced the wall dividing her from the man she loved. Wiping away the tears of happiness, she wished she could share the moment with Jake.

Instead, Krista pulled out the drawer of the desk to find a Bible. She took it and began leafing through the pages. Retreating to her bed, she pulled the pillows out from under the spread and propped herself up. The accounts of men and women of God came to life as she read.

It was hours later when she heard a knock at her door. She opened it to a bleary-eyed, sheepish looking Jake.

"I didn't mean to sleep so long," he said as he stood in the doorway. "Are you all right?"

She smiled, stepping outside the door to stand with him in the late afternoon sun. "I'm better than all right, Jake. I had a long talk with my *Lord*, and asked God to forgive me for my selfishness. . .my willfulness."

The smile that transformed Jake's face was wonderful for Krista to behold.

"Praise God!" Jake exclaimed. Krista found herself in his arms. He was laughing with delight. "You can't imagine how much I've prayed for you about that. Truly God is good!"

Krista was laughing with Jake. "I'm so glad, too, Jake. I never would have believed the joy and release I've felt. I've been reading," Krista added, glancing quickly through the open doorway toward where she had been sitting. "There was a Bible in the desk drawer. I never realized the Bible could be so fascinating. But those were real people with real faults and troubles. Some of them had a hard time letting God lead them where He wanted them to go. Yet, I saw that when they trusted Him, believed Him—obeyed Him, He blessed them. I have so much to learn. Teach me, Jake? Help me to understand who God wants me to be. I want to grow in my knowledge of the Lord, to use my life for Him."

"As do I," Jake murmured lovingly.

Krista stared into Jake's piney-green eyes and saw the love reflected there. She basked in his gaze, searching his face. Why this man should love her. . . .

"Krista, . . ." Jake said, taking both of her hands in his.

"Yes."

"This is probably not the most romantic spot we could be in."

Krista's heart paused as she returned his slow, mischievous gleam.

"I could think of others. . ." Krista returned, unable to resist, with a serious lightness of her own.

"You know that I love you."

Krista nodded.

Jake looked deeply into Krista's soft, grey eyes. "If you could possibly consider sharing your life with me, would you marry me, Krista?"

"Knowing that you love me and that we both have the Lord Jesus directing our lives makes me happier than I've ever been, Jake. Yes," she nodded, "I'd like very much to be Mrs. Jake McIntyre."

—25—

Krista reached back inside her car and drew out the pile of mail Jake had put there earlier. The Colorado sun poured its autumn warmth on her back and Krista straightened, swinging her hair back out of her face.

Jake's friend had been very generous in offering to let her stay at his secluded home while he and his wife were on an extended vacation. Krista enjoyed the peaceful solitude, but she missed her own home...and McIntyres'. Jake had kept her sequestered here for the past five weeks, and she was beginning to chaff at the restriction. She had just now returned from her first visit to the restaurant since their arrival home. She could empathize with his concern—after all, it was her life they were protecting. *But still . . .*

Krista sighed and shuffled through the mail as she climbed the steps to the front door. There was the usual assortment of junk mail, besides a thick packet from her lawyer, and, surprisingly, deep in the pile, a letter from Jennifer. Curiously, Krista inspected the turquoise envelope. It had been mailed from Hawaii.

On impluse Krista detoured around the side of the house to the back patio where she dropped her armload on a small table. She sat down on the suspended swing and idly set the chair in motion. She could not help but wonder what had become of Jennifer after the airport.

Quickly Krista scanned the contents of the letter, and gasped in surprise—Jennifer and Broderick had eloped and were spending their honeymoon in Hawaii! Jennifer's letter

178

included Broderick's apologies for his threats and rash actions.

Krista's hands dropped to her lap, folding the sheets between her fingers.

Broderick had gotten his heiress. She remembered the hastily scrawled note he had left at the estate. A chill crept up her spine. If the attempts on her life hadn't been a result of Broderick's jealousy. . .then *who*. . .?

Sliding the sheets inside the envelope, Krista shifted the load of mail and juggled her key ring to find the one that matched the lock on the patio doors. Jake planned to come for dinner, and she wanted to make it a special evening. Last night they had set the date for their wedding.

Krista placed the key in the lock—and it turned as if the lock had already been undone. She shrugged. It was probably her imagination. There were so many things on her mind.

The door slid silently shut behind her, and Krista inspected the thick envelope from Uncle Anthony's lawyer. It would take time to review its contents. There was much for her to consider. . .so many possible options.

Krista's footsteps made little whispering sounds on the hardwood floor as she bypassed the eating area and turned to take her things to the guest room. A movement out of the corner of her eye caused her to glance into the vaulted living room.

Her breath caught in her throat.

"Steven! How did you get in?" Then, as her grip tightened on the articles she carried, "What. . .do you want?"

Steven shifted his position on the sofa and adjusted one of the many embroidered throw pillows to a more comfortable spot. He gave a smile of relief and said quite simply, "Money," the word rolling off his tongue with delicious ease.

"How did you find me?"

"I followed your Mr. McIntyre here last night. I arrived earlier this afternoon only to find you weren't home, so I let myself in. You really should be more careful about locking all the doors, Krista. You wouldn't want just anyone walking in—especially with whispered rumors of someone endangering your life." His fingers fluttered, "Ah, the peril of being horrendously wealthy. Someone will always try to take it for himself."

"Like you?" Krista asked, her chin rising in a measured, deliberate motion as she studied her cousin with widened eyes. "It *was* you—in the car, at the pool, through my window. Money. . .that's been the whole idea all along, hasn't it? That's why you tried to kill me—so you could have the Mariano fortune. Without me around you would inherit it all."

Steven's head shook tolerantly. Taking one of the pillows beside him, he twirled it between his flattened hands.

Steven's mouth twisted sideways. "Linda told me what you said that night you left so. . .precipitously. You always were one to jump to conclusions about me, Krista. Granted, I was upset over the outcome of the will. I was—am still—in need of finances to bail me out of a difficult situation. But, contrary to your fanciful assumption, I am not a murderer."

"Of course it wasn't him. It was me."

Krista turned violently at the passive, soft-spoken voice. Steven stiffened, dark eyes expanding as he focused on the person behind her.

Nan.

The housekeeper was calmly holding a small pistol in her hand.

"You?" Krista breathed hoarsely. "But *why?*"

Fear pierced Krista as she watched Nan casually hold the deadly weapon on her.

"Why?" Nan repeated, her eyes beginning to glitter as her face drew taut with unexpressed emotion. "Because of you—and what you did. You never cared about anyone other than yourself. You never considered how Anthony felt and how he loved you. *You* killed Anthony. If it had not been for you, he would still be alive, filling my days with generosity and kindness. He worried about you. His worry caused his illness." Her fingers whitened around the small gun. "It was your final rejection that killed him."

Krista's mouth slackened. Stricken by the words Nan uttered, she could only stare at the woman.

"You would not come home," Nan continued. "That was all he asked. . .so he could see you again."

Steven's voice, a thin sound, broke Nan's tirade. "You know that's not true, Nan. Uncle Anthony died of cancer. He'd been sick for years."

"He died of a broken heart!" Nan snarled and turned the gun at Steven. Krista gasped. Steven blanched, his fingers stabbing the pillow he held in his hands.

Nan stopped, composed herself, then redirected her aim and attention back to Krista. "I tried to have you eliminated before you could sully the name of your uncle."

"The car. . ." Krista breathed.

Nan managed a tight smile. "When that did not work, I took matters into my own hands. Did you seriously think," Nan questioned, "that I would allow you to deny the Mariano legacy and then—and then to let you turn Anthony's gracious home into a girl's school? The Mariano Estate is a treasure to be cherished by those who can truly understand what it is a symbol of—not by ungrateful waifs such as yourself." Her eyes widened fractionally. "I almost succeeded. If only you had drunk the coffee the night your gentleman friend came. I would have succeeded at the pool, too, if your gentleman friend had not been so quick to come to your rescue. It is too bad, really. He seems to be such a nice young man. He will miss you sorely, I am afraid. . .much like I miss Anthony."

"You're crazy," Krista said, staring at Nan. There was a perfect, dark round hole in the end of the gun. Krista trembled, clutching her letters and purse close to her heart, as if the action could somehow stop the force of a bullet.

"No," the woman denied, "only determined to accomplish what I came to do."

"What. . .about me?" Steven managed to ask, having straightened to the edge of the sofa. His tan was a sickly yellow. His fingers gripped the pillow tightly.

"You," Nan's head shook as she motioned Krista to move closer to Steven. Krista jerked at the gun's movement. Nan stepped further into the room. "You always were a problem—wrecking my plans when I least expected it . . . . Although this time you did me quite a service, keeping me informed, letting me know when you found Krista. I must admit to some concern as I saw the weeks passing without a sign of her. I had originally intended to do this for you, to keep a Mariano in the home, but now I see that will not be possible. I cannot have you telling the police that I shot Krista."

"Then why kill us?" Krista asked. Her mind was working furiously. "If you shoot both of us, no Mariano will inherit, and the estate will go to strangers."

"It will go to me." An unholy light gleamed from Nan's eyes. "Surprised? There was an addendum to the will—in the letter Anthony left for me. He asked me to keep it quiet so the two of you would not be prejudiced against me if I chose to remain in my position at the estate. He knew how I loved my job, how I loved to work in his home." Nan focused on Krista's clutching hands, on the large envelope with the lawyer's name plainly evident. "All that work Mr. Wood and Mr. Canterbury have gone to. . . ." Her head shook as she made a noise, ". . .all for naught. It will be a surprise to everyone. When both of you die, I inherit. It should have gone to me anyway. I deserved it. I loved Anthony. . .and he loved me. Neither of you cared."

"You'll never get away with this," Krista said.

"Of course I will. I have it all planned." She glanced toward Steven. "With a few modifications."

"The police will check up on you," Steven said. "They'll find out you were here."

"It will be a case of mistaken identity. You see, Aunt Miriam will testify that I've been at her home all week, on my vacation. She is so simple minded, and she trusts me explicitly. She will believe me when I tell her I arrived yesterday. I will remind her of all the things we have done, and she will agree, fabricating the stories in her mind until she actually believes something that never occurred."

"You *are* crazy," Steven said.

Nan merely stared at him. "It is time we get this over with. I have a plane to catch, and I do not want to miss my flight. I think what we will do," Nan considered, "is have a murder/suicide. Steven, you came to plead for money for your gambling debts and when Krista refused, in the heat of the moment, you shot her. I heard," Nan interjected, "what you said in the library. When the police ask, I will recall that you did threaten violence to retrieve yourself from the pit of your debts. Then," she continued, "when you realized what you had done to your cousin, you found you could not live with that, so you shot yourself.

"Yes," Nan studied the wide-eyed pair in front of her. "I think that will do nicely. Steven, very carefully stand and go to that desk over there." She indicated an oak rolltop desk placed against the wall. "I am certain you will find writing paper there. You must leave a convincing note for the people who will find you."

"You can't do this," Steven said, his fingers compulsively twisting and tugging at the pillow. "You can't just kill us and act as if you are on a picnic."

"I am not on a picnic," Nan corrected him. "I'm on vacation. Now, *go!*" Her expression altered as she jerked the pistol toward Steven.

As Steven began to rise, Krista cried out in desperation, "No!"

Nan flung her aim back toward Krista and Krista threw up

her hands, mail and purse flying out and cascading to the floor.

In that split second, Steven spun the pillow he held in his hands at Nan.

Nan gave an exclamation of surprise, instinctively jerking her hands up to ward off the blow. Steven jumped at that instant, slamming his shoulder into Nan's midsection, throwing her to the ground.

Nan's scream was an unearthly cry. A shot rang out, smacking the ceiling. Krista screamed, staring helplessly at the two people on the floor. Steven fought to hold Nan's arm, managing to snare her wrist with his left hand. Another shot thudded into the wall.

Nan fought like a madwoman, the fingers of her free hand clawing at Steven, ripping at his hair.

Steven lifted and smashed Nan's hand to the floor, loosening her grip on the gun. Once more, and the pistol went spinning across the hardwood planking.

Krista snatched at the gun, recoiling from the feel of its weight in her hand, then leapt past Steven and Nan. Someone—Jake—was pounding on the front door.

"*Krista!*" Jake yelled, dashing through the door as Krista flung it open.

Krista gave a sobbing exclamation of relief and threw herself into his arms. He squeezed her for a brief moment, then gave Krista a deliberate push toward the kitchen. "Call the police!" he ordered as he swung himself toward the struggling pair. Together he and Steven succeeded in capturing Nan's free hand, pinning the writhing woman and forcing her to the floor. Her face was an ugly mask of hate, her screams horrible.

With a backward glance, Krista sped to do as Jake instructed. She dropped the pistol on the counter with a sharp cry of distaste. Her trembling fingers were barely able to tap out 9-1-1.

—26—

Carrie straightened Krista's cascading veil and smiled at the bride. "You look absolutely beautiful!" she said.

Krista beamed. She felt utterly, deliciously beautiful. In a few short minutes she would become Mrs. Jake Lee McIntyre.

There was a light rapping at the door.

"Is it time?" Krista questioned anxiously, twirling to face the doorway. Her insides fluttered at the thought. She pushed at the flowing skirt of her gown, smoothing the white satin and lace with nervous hands.

Linda peered around the door. "It's just me," she said. "Could I. . .talk with you for a moment?"

Krista smiled. "Come on in," she said, drawing Linda into the room.

"I'll go see how much longer it'll be before we start," Carrie offered. She left with a rustle of blue silk and the lingering scent of pink roses from the bouquet she lifted from the table as she moved.

Linda looked. . .happy. A faint blush gave an attractive tint to her pretty face.

"I just. . .wanted to thank you," Linda said, "for all you have done for Steven."

"I have a lot to thank Steven for," Krista returned. "If it wasn't for him, neither of us would be here today."

"But to loan him the money to pay his debts? You know he's going to Gamblers Anonymous?"

"So I was told. I'm very glad for both of you."

"He proposed, too." Linda held out her left hand for Krista to see the modest solitaire. "It's all paid for. He sold some of his things," she explained. "He's making plans for a business, too. I think he's going to do real well. . .thanks to you."

"No," Krista denied, "thanks to Steven. He'll pull through just fine. He's a Mariano. Marianos have fortitude and good business sense. . .once they decide to use it." Her last words were tempered with a smile.

"There's just. . .one other thing. . . ."

"What is it?" Krista asked in concern as she saw Linda's brow knit with a tiny furrow.

"It may seem silly. . .and certainly it's nothing that I should bother you with on your wedding day. . .but I feel it's very important that I talk to you about it. I know you're going to be leaving right after the reception and with all the people here we'll never have a chance to really. . .talk."

"Go on," Krista prompted.

Linda paused. "I noticed in California how different you seemed to be from your family. And I've noticed since we've been here the past couple of days the. . .peace you've had about that horrible ordeal with Nan. And after all that I've heard about the way your uncle demanded so much of you, yet. . .you have a forgiving attitude that I don't understand. Steven says you've changed. What, if I can ask," she ventured cautiously, "caused that difference? Steven says it's because you're getting married. I said. . .there's another reason."

Krista's heart filled with joy at Linda's question. *Thank you, Lord Jesus, for this opportunity to pass on what you've given to me.*

"There is," Krista assured her. "Jesus Christ is that reason."

There was a tap at the door.

Linda appeared perplexed.

Carrie poked her head through the doorway and said, "Time to go!"

"I'll be right there," Krista answered with a wave of her hand. To Linda she said, "Jesus Christ, God's Son, forgave me for every sin—every hatred and wrong thought I ever had, and gave me the strength to forgive others. Because of Him, and because I've let Him be Lord of my life, I have peace."

"Krista!" came Carrie's entreating voice as she poked her head into the room once more. "Jake's waiting! Darrell's playing the most gorgeous music; he called it 'Krista's Song'."

"Okay. . .I'm coming!" Krista answered.

"Forgive me. . ." Linda started to apologize for bothering Krista.

"No, there's nothing to forgive! It's wonderful that you asked. We'll talk." Krista snatched her bouquet. "Later, after the ceremony," she promised. As they walked out the door, Krista saw Jake looking at her, waiting to walk her down the aisle. She smiled at the love bursting in her heart as she turned to Linda. "I want to tell you about a wonderful free gift that will change your life. . .forever."